She stopped in fr

stopped with her.

"This is me." Her voice sounded husky. She cleared her throat and tried to ignore the pulse rushing in her ears. "Thanks for walking me to the door."

He pointed to the door across from hers. "This is me. I guess we're neighbors."

Heaven help her, he was across the hall. She swallowed hard. "I guess so."

He reached over and touched her hair. Vanessa sucked in a breath as his fingers slid through her hair. His fingers didn't touch her skin, but the heat of his body singed her. The spicy scent of his cologne enticed her.

He pulled back with a white piece of lint between his fingers. "You had something in your hair." The deep rumble of his voice vibrated across her skin.

"Oh. I thought you were trying to flirt with me."

His lips lifted in a sexy smile. "You'll know when I'm trying to flirt with you." He gave her one last heated look before he turned to his door.

Dear Reader,

I'm a low-key lover of things paranormal and spooky, so needless to say, when I ran across the show *Ghost Brothers* one day, I immediately knew I had to write a story about three ghost-investigating brothers.

Summoning Up Love is the first installment in my new series inspired by that day of channel surfing. It's not a paranormal romance series, but one that introduces you to three handsome brothers who've taken their curiosity about ghosts and turned it into an interesting side hustle. A side hustle I would love to do myself, but I don't know if I have enough time to fit in paranormal investigator with my romance writing.

I hope you enjoy my Heart & Soul series. Be sure to reach out to me on social media or by email and let me know what you think. I always love connecting with readers.

Happy reading,

Synithia

Summoning Up Love

SYNITHIA WILLIAMS

HARLEQUIN
SPECIAL
EDITION

Recycling programs
for this product may
not exist in your area.

ISBN-13: 978-1-335-40851-8

Summoning Up Love

Harlequin Enterprises ULC
22 Adelaide St. West, 41st Floor
Toronto, Ontario M5H 4E3, Canada
www.Harlequin.com

Printed in U.S.A.

Synithia Williams has been an avid romance-novel lover since picking up her first at the age of thirteen. It was only natural that she would begin penning her own romances soon after—much to the chagrin of her high school math teachers. She's a native of South Carolina and now writes romances as hot as their Southern settings. Outside of writing she works on water quality and sustainability issues for local government. She's married to her own personal hero, and they have two sons, who've convinced her that professional wrestling and superheroes are supreme entertainment. When she isn't working, writing, or being a wife and mother, she's usually bingeing on TV series, playing around on social media or planning her next girls' night out with friends. You can learn more about Synithia by visiting her website, www.synithiawilliams.com.

Books by Synithia Williams

Harlequin Special Edition

Heart & Souls

Summoning Up Love

HQN

Jackson Falls

The Promise of a Kiss
Forbidden Promises
Scandalous Secrets
Careless Whispers
Foolish Hearts

Visit the Author Profile page
at Harlequin.com for more titles.

Chapter One

At least I can hide at the beach.

The phrase had brushed across Vanessa's mind repeatedly during the five-hour car ride from Atlanta. Now, as she pulled her rental into the drive of the small cottage where she'd seek refuge for a few months, she waited for the relief to ease the tension in her shoulders and the knots in her stomach.

Relief did not appear. The emotion must have decided to take notes from her ex-boyfriend and abandon her.

Still, the beachside cottage was someplace to hide. Thank God she had that. She didn't have to stay in Atlanta, where all her friends and colleagues—wait, former colleagues—would give her sad looks and insist she "get back out there." Here, she could take her time feeling sorry for herself in private.

"Nope, not feeling sorry for myself," she whispered as she cut the engine to the small sedan. "Things could have been worse."

So what if she'd gotten fired and dumped on the same day. Who cares that she'd expected a promotion instead of a pink slip when the news director scheduled a meeting with her after the morning broadcast. So what if her boyfriend hadn't technically dumped her, but instead insisted they "go on a break" the same day she'd been fired because his horoscope said he shouldn't make any major commitments. She still had her health, right?

Vanessa's shoulders slumped. Internal pep talk failure. The past week had been horrible, and while she was well aware there were worse things happening in the world, she deserved a few days to be in her feelings. Maybe a few weeks.

She opened the door and got out of the vehicle. The late fall afternoon was humid and windy. The smell of the not-so-distant ocean brought a small smile to her face. She hadn't been here since the summer she turned thirteen, but it still felt like coming home. She left her bags in the car and went up the sturdy wooden stairs to the front door of the single-story white home.

A wave of memories washed over her after she entered the house. Summers in Sunshine Beach, South Carolina were some of her happiest memories. She could hear the echo of her and her baby sister Jada's footsteps on the hardwood floors as they ran from the front door through the house out back to the beach. See the indoor campground they'd make in the living room to watch scary movies while eating big bowls of popcorn, grilled hot dogs and multiple types of chips.

For the first time since that horrible day the tightness in her chest eased.

Yes, Sunshine Beach was the best place to get her life back together. This was just another bump on the road to success. She'd find a job even better than the one she lost, Daniel would come to his senses and try to make up, but she was done with him. She was focused on finding a way to bounce back.

She went back outside and got her bags out of the car. It didn't take long to put her clothes and other personal items in the master bedroom. As she organized her toiletries in the bathroom, a loud thump came from somewhere in the house. Vanessa froze and listened. Several seconds passed with no other noise. She continued unpacking when the thump came again.

"What in the world…" she murmured to herself. She left the bathroom and stood in the middle of the bedroom. The wind blew harder outside. The house creaked and moaned with each heavy gust. Before driving to Sunshine Beach, she'd checked the weather report. A storm was coming in overnight, which was why she'd driven practically nonstop to get there before nightfall.

A third thump came from the back of the house. Vanessa jumped at the unexpected and loud sound. Sighing with frustration, she left the bedroom and headed toward the kitchen. If the winds from the incoming storm were knocking something against the house, then she needed to find out what and tie it down. She'd lost enough sleep the past few nights thanks to the changing situation in her life. She didn't need to lose more precious sleep from bumps in the night.

She went to the back door that connected the kitchen to the screened-in porch. She reached for the knob, but it twisted slowly before she touched it. Her heart jumped and she jerked back. Sunshine Beach was a relatively safe town. The idea of an intruder coming hadn't even crossed her mind. But she'd reported enough home invasion stories in her career to realize no town, no matter how idealistic, was without its share of bad people.

Her grandmother said the house hadn't been rented in weeks. Someone could know that and decided tonight was the night to break in and take what they wanted. Before she could tamp down the anxiety that accompanied that thought, the door opened. A burst of warm, humid air blew inside.

Vanessa hopped back and let out a high-pitched shriek.

"What in the world are you yelling for?" An older woman's voice cut off Vanessa's panic.

Vanessa placed a hand over her racing heart. "Grandma, what are you doing here?"

Arletha Montgomery shook her head as she came into the kitchen, her dark eyes sparkling with humor. Short, plump, with tawny brown skin that had a few laugh lines around her eyes and mouth, Arletha's welcoming personality always filled up a room.

"I'm here to check on you. What do you think I'm doing here?" her grandmother said as if that were obvious. She tugged on the front of her bright yellow jacket. "That still doesn't explain why you're yelling."

"I heard a thump and then the door suddenly opened on its own." Vanessa heard how ridiculous her statement sounded.

"I didn't realize you were so scared," Arletha said, chuckling.

Vanessa straightened her shoulders. She tried to look stern, but her lips twitched. "I'm not scared, Grandma. I am cautious. Besides, I thought you'd come to the front door."

Arletha waved a hand. "I would have, but the wind is picking up and I haven't fixed the latch on the screened porch. I decided to tie it down before saying hello. That's the thump you probably heard."

"Thank you for that."

Arletha shrugged. "I'll get someone to come replace the latch. Until then, remember to keep the door tied closed. We're expecting thunderstorms tonight and tomorrow. The last thing I need is for the door to fly away."

Arletha walked past Vanessa toward the front of the house. "Do you need any help moving in?"

Vanessa followed her grandmother into the living area. "No, I've got all of my stuff out of the car. I'm unpacking now."

"Good. If you need anything, let me know. I'm happy to have you here. I just wish it were under better circumstances."

Her grandmother looked around the living room as she spoke. Inspecting the windows, pillows on the couches and the fireplace. Vanessa sat on the edge of the couch and let her grandmother do her usual inspection. Arletha was proud of owning multiple properties in Sunshine Beach and worked hard to keep them in top shape. Vanessa was surprised the latch on the back door hadn't been replaced already.

"So do I," she replied.

"I can't believe they fired you! You were the best person at that station."

Vanessa smiled despite the pain. Her family had been so happy when she'd started her job as a beat reporter for Atlanta's largest news network. In six years she'd gone from beat reporter to morning news host and sometimes evening fill-in. The reviews when she did fill in were consistently high, so when the previous evening news host retired, Vanessa had assumed she would be chosen for the position.

"They're going in a new direction," Vanessa said, making air quotes with her fingers.

Arletha stopped checking the window locks and turned back to Vanessa. "New direction? What better direction than to have the smartest, funniest, most beautiful person at that station be the face of the evening news?"

"That was exactly the problem." Vanessa's shoulders slumped. "The new GM wants to focus on more hard-line stories."

"We're sure you'll find a great position more suitable to your talents." The new general manager's words whispered through Vanessa's head. He'd never said it, and had gone above and beyond reassuring her that she was a talented anchor, but Vanessa knew what the problem was. They wanted hard-hitting, investigative reporting, not the bubbly community-focused stories the station was known for. The stories Vanessa had built her career on.

Along with the positive reviews were also the negative. The complaints that Vanessa's dresses were "too sexy" or "too revealing" even when she and one of the thinner, less curvy anchors wore something similar. That her long curly hair was a distraction whenever she alternated her style. Worse than that were the comments from a few creeps about all the things they'd like to do to her in graphic detail.

"Why can't you do hard-line stories?" her grandmother asked.

"I can, but they don't agree. But you know what, it'll be okay. I'll find another job and it'll be better than the one I had." She infused her voice with optimism. If she believed she'd bounce back, then she would. She couldn't believe she'd fail. Couldn't believe other stations would only see her as a sexy desk candy, as one former coworker had called her. Couldn't believe she wouldn't bounce back bigger and better.

Arletha raised a hand to the sky. "Go ahead and claim it." She crossed the room and placed a hand on Vanessa's shoulder. "Take all the time you need here."

"What about your rentals?"

"The summer is over, and fall isn't nearly as busy. Even if it were the middle of summer, I'd find a way for you to stay. Figure out your next steps, relax and come up with a game plan."

Vanessa smiled and took a deep breath. She was grateful to have her grandmother's support. "I will."

Her grandmother shook her shoulder. "And don't think about that fool Daniel, either. You dodged a bullet with that one."

Vanessa held up a hand. "Let's not talk about Daniel right now."

Her family was pissed, but his asking for a break shouldn't have surprised her. Daniel was incredibly superstitious and would completely uproot his entire schedule if his horoscope or numerology said he needed to change something. The breakup was a good thing. They could've gotten married and had three kids before his horoscope told him to move on with his life. She'd look on the bright side and ignore the pain of knowing he hadn't loved her enough to overlook a few words sent to him via an astrology app on his phone.

"Fine. We won't talk about him." Her grand-mother checked her watch. "Well, I won't stay in your way. I've got to get back to the house anyway. I've got some people coming over."

Vanessa's eyes widened. She didn't want her grandmother to leave. The idea of being alone in the house made her anxious. Not from the scare, but because being alone left her too much time to think about what was wrong in her life. Her grandmother's enthusiasm was what she needed right now. "Who's coming over?" Maybe she could butt in on the visit.

Her grandmother avoided eye contact and waved a hand. "Some local guys, you don't know them, but they've agreed to help me out."

"Is something wrong at the house?"

Arletha opened and then closed her mouth. She peered at Vanessa out of the corner of her eye. Vanessa raised her brows and waited.

"It's your grandfather."

Vanessa blinked several times. "Granddad?" she asked, confused. Her grandfather passed a year ago.

Arletha let out a long breath and said in a rush, "He's haunting the place and I want to know why."

Vanessa blinked slowly. Her head tilted to the side as she took a moment to process the words. Her grandmother didn't smile or say she was joking.

"Say what now?"

"He's haunting the place, so I've asked the Livingston boys to figure out why. Maybe if I can give him peace he'll go on his way." She turned toward the door.

Vanessa jumped up from the couch. "Grandma, hold on. You can't be serious right now." There was no way her grandmother could say something so outrageous and just walk out.

"I'm very serious. That's what the Livingston Boys do. They get to the bottom of things like this and I hired them to help me."

"Hold up. *Hired?*" Vanessa's scam alert sensors went off. Who were these guys anyway? "You're paying for this?"

Arletha patted Vanessa's shoulder. "It's all good. Just finish unpacking, and I'll let you know what I find out tomorrow." Her grandmother reached for the door.

Vanessa's hand shot out and wrapped around her grandmother's elbow. "Oh no. This won't wait until tomorrow. I'm coming with you." She snatched up her purse from the couch. There were no such things as ghosts, and her grandfather damn sure wasn't one. No way was she going to let some scammers prey on her grandmother. She was getting to the bottom of this.

"Now, Vanessa—"

"No, Grandma, you're not talking me out of this. I'm going to find out what's going on tonight."

Chapter Two

Vanessa ignored her grandmother's insistence that she was overreacting as they drove the ten minutes to her grandmother's two-story, colonial-style home. When her grandfather was alive, her grandparents had used the home as a bed-and-breakfast and rented out rooms on the second floor. After his passing, her grandmother closed the bed-and-breakfast, saying it wasn't the same without Lou around and that she made enough money renting the houses they'd acquired over the years so the lost income wouldn't hurt.

Vanessa had worried her grandmother would be lonely without her grandfather or frequent guests to keep her company. Her mom insisted everything would be okay. Whenever she called, her grandmother was in good spirits and had found ways to keep herself busy working part-time at city hall and her monthly book club meetings. Vanessa never would have guessed her grandmother was so lonely she'd imagine her husband was haunting the house or that she'd go so far as to trust some random wackos to investigate.

Vanessa didn't feel an ounce of shame for judging the men. Anyone who would prey on an elderly woman who missed her late husband deserved to be called much worse. She could just imagine the dudes coming to do the so-called investigation. Some tech-loving conspiracy theorists, with wild hair and a bunch of fake instruments that buzzed and lit up. They'd throw out pseudoscientific words that made no sense to dazzle their clients with their "knowledge."

Not today, and not with her grandmother. The higher-ups at the Atlanta News Network may not think she was "serious" enough to handle investigative journalism, but she'd interviewed enough professional scammers and researched enough shady stories to know when someone was trying to run a hoax.

"You're overreacting," her grandmother said when they turned onto her street. "It's that reporter brain of yours. Everyone isn't a criminal, child."

"Yeah, well, we shall see," Vanessa grumbled.

A steel gray pickup truck was parked in the driveway. Her grandmother's eyes lit up and she grinned. "Oh, great, they're already here. Now don't you go starting something. Let the boys do what they do and leave them alone."

"The boys?" Vanessa looked from her grandmother to the pickup truck. "Grandma, they're driving a big truck. They're not boys." More like grown men out to make a quick hustle.

"I've known the Livingston boys since they were teenagers. They're going to always be boys to me. Your grandfather really liked them. Just be quiet and keep an open mind."

Vanessa pursed her lips instead of responding. The fact that these "boys" knew her grandfather only made Vanessa doubt them more. They had to know how much her grandmother missed her husband and that's why they'd chosen to make her a target.

Arletha pulled her burgundy Buick LaCrosse next to the truck. The windows were tinted so Vanessa couldn't size up the "boys" inside. After they got out of the car, her grandmother rushed around the car waving and smiling.

"Sorry I'm late, boys. I had to check on my granddaughter."

Vanessa crossed her arms and glared at the truck. She'd been itching for a fight since getting fired. Who knew she'd get the chance to take out her frustration so perfectly? The truck doors opened, and three fine-as-hell *men* stepped out.

Her jaw dropped. She couldn't help it. She hadn't

expected them to be good-looking. Sleazy guys shouldn't be good-looking.

Guy number one stood on the driver's side. He was the tallest of the three with chestnut brown skin, a smooth bald head and a neat goatee framing full lips. He wore a plain gray sweatshirt, dark jeans and boots. The guy scanned the scene, her and her grandmother with a sharp, efficient gaze. She immediately assessed he was the leader.

Guy number two stood on the passenger side. Same skin tone, but with thick curly hair tapered in a stylish fade, and a dazzling smile. His slim-fit joggers and black-and-gold shirt were just as stylish as his hair. Definitely the pretty boy of the group.

Guy number three stood on the back passenger side. He was the slimmest of the three, with a low-cut fade, bedroom eyes and a full beard. A light yellow shirt made his dark skin glow and fitted jeans encased his long legs. He gave a shy smile as he stood just behind the pretty boy. He deferred to the others, but his straight shoulders and direct stare meant he wasn't to be underestimated.

Definitely not what I expected.

They all grinned and exchanged pleasantries as they greeted and hugged her grandmother. By the time her grandmother brought them over to her, she'd gotten some of her bearings together. So what if they were the embodiment of a thirst trap? That didn't mean they weren't terrible people.

Vanessa snapped herself back to the reason she'd

come in the first place. To look out for her grandmother. For all she knew these guys had dazzled
her grandmother with their equally winning smiles
and that's why she'd agreed to this ridiculous thing.

"Vanessa, this is Dion." She pointed to guy number one. "Tyrone." Guy number two. "And Wesley."
Guy number three. "Boys, this is my granddaughter Vanessa."

Dion stepped forward and held out a hand. When
he smiled, dimples appeared in his cheeks. The air
rushed out of her lungs.

"Hello, Vanessa, it's nice to meet you."

That. Damn. Voice! Deep, rich and smoother than
melted chocolate. A shiver went down her spine. For
half a second, she felt a ridiculous urge to giggle and
push the hair behind her ears.

Her back stiffened. Now she understood why her
grandmother had gone along with this foolishness.
These guys were walking fantasies with charming
smiles and dimples to boot. No way was she going
to fall for the okey-doke.

Vanessa crossed her arms over her chest and lifted
her chin. "So you're the guys trying to take advantage of my grandmother."

Dion's smile stiffened. He curled his hand in and
pulled back. So that's how this was going to go. Frustration prickled across his skin, but he wouldn't let it
show. Vanessa wasn't the first person to come at him
and his brothers that way and she wouldn't be the

last. Plus, he respected Mrs. Montgomery too much to return her granddaughter's rudeness with his own.

"Vanessa!" Mrs. Montgomery rushed forward and poked Vanessa's shoulder. "Don't be rude."

Dion held up his hands. "It's okay, Mrs. Montgomery." He looked back at Vanessa. "I promise you we aren't here to take advantage of anyone."

He gave her his winning smile. The one he used at the day job when talking to angry citizens who wanted the pothole on their street repaired immediately but his crew couldn't get to it for a few days. That smile typically got him a begrudging acknowledgment that he was trying to help, and a few notes to his director expressing gratitude.

For a second, he thought the smile would work on Vanessa. The ice in her eyes thawed slightly and the corner of her mouth quivered as if she were about to smile. Then she blinked and straightened her shoulders. The frost returned with more force. Okay, he'd have to work harder to get off her bad side.

"I'll be the judge of that," she said stiffly.

Despite the stiff tone, her voice did something weird to his insides. It was soft and husky, bringing visions of lazy mornings in bed, legs entwined, skin to skin. Dion swallowed hard and shifted back. He'd dealt with diffusing the situation with difficult people for years and one of the cardinal rules was to never let his libido get involved in the discussion. Vanessa was gorgeous. Golden brown skin, thick wavy hair, big dark eyes and curves straight out of his fantasies. But if he gave any indication of his immediate, visceral and primal attraction to her, then things would go from difficult to downright disastrous.

"That's why we're here. Whatever questions you have we'll answer," he said in his best help-me-help-you voice.

"See, Vanessa, I told you Dion and his brothers were nice guys." Mrs. Montgomery smiled at Dion. "You boys want to come in?"

Dion nodded. "Sure." He took a step toward the house. Wes and Tyrone came forward.

Vanessa slid to the left and blocked his path. Her brown eyes sparked with suspicion. "Hold up. What exactly are you going inside for?"

Tyrone, always impatient, came up beside Dion. "To check out the house and talk to Mrs. Montgomery about what she's experienced."

Vanessa's eyes narrowed. "What she's experienced is a group of hustlers trying to get something out of her."

Tyrone pointed a finger. "Hold up. What you ain't gonna do—"

Dion raised his hand. Tyrone pressed his lips together and stepped back. "Tyrone, it's cool." His brother gave him a sharp look, but he backed down. He met Vanessa's eyes. "Look, I understand you don't know us, and this may sound strange."

"Strange and unrealistic," Vanessa snapped, and gave a little neck twist that was hella sexy.

Mrs. Montgomery huffed. "Will you stop giving the guys a hard time? At least let them come in and talk."

"No, Grandma. This whole haunting thing is nonsense. And they aren't here to investigate and tell you what's going on."

Dion bit back a sigh. "Mrs. Montgomery, why don't we come back another day?" He didn't know Vanessa, but he didn't think pushing this today was going to get him any brownie points. From what Mrs. Montgomery told him, she was some hotshot reporter in Atlanta. She was probably in town for a few days to visit. Instead of arguing with her, he'd wait until she was out of town and talk to Mrs. Montgomery.

Despite what Vanessa thought of them, he and his brothers believed people when they said something wasn't right in their homes. They checked things out, discovered what was going on and offered solutions to help people feel more comfortable in their homes. They weren't exorcists, priests or scammers. They were just three regular guys who had seen enough to believe sometimes the ancestors still had things to say.

Mrs. Montgomery threw a frustrated look at Vanessa before nodding. "That's a good idea. Vanessa just got into town, so this is all new and sudden to her."

Dion glanced at Vanessa. "I hope you'll feel more comfortable about everything before you leave."

"Oh, I'm not going anywhere," Vanessa replied

with a smug gleam in her eye. As if she'd read his thoughts and knew he planned to wait her out.

"Vanessa is staying at my rental on Spring Street for a few weeks," Mrs. Montgomery explained.

The smug gleam turned into a smug smile. "Which means I'll have plenty of time to watch you and make sure you don't do anything to hurt my grandmother."

Tyrone scoffed. "Ma'am, I promise you we don't want to hurt Mrs. Montgomery."

Vanessa's sharp gaze zeroed in on his younger brother. Dion shifted to bring her attention back to him. "My brother's right. Since you're in town, that gives you more time to get to know us." He reached into his back pocket and pulled out a business card. "Here, take this. After you've talked this over with Mrs. Montgomery some more, give me a call. I'm happy to answer any of your questions."

She snatched the card out of his hand and eyed it like a radioactive specimen. "Oh, believe me, I will get all of my questions answered."

Her adamant defense of her grandmother was admirable. The way she pursed her full lips and the whiff of her perfume the wind drifted his way brought that weird feeling back to his stomach. Time to go before things got worse. "I know you will." He glanced at Mrs. Montgomery. "Have a good evening, Mrs. Montgomery. Give us a call when you want us to come back."

Mrs. Montgomery gave him a tight, apologetic smile. "I will, Dion. Thank you for coming by."

They smiled and nodded at Mrs. Montgomery before getting back in his truck. As soon as they backed out of the driveway, his brothers went in.

"Can you believe that?" Tyrone said from the passenger seat. "She looked at us like we are really some hustlers. What was up with that? We wouldn't hurt Mrs. Montgomery."

"She doesn't know us," Dion said evenly. His brother could go from zero to sixty in no time flat, but claimed he was the least emotional of the three. Dion had played the level head for his younger brother for most of his life. "Of course she's going to look out for her grandmother."

Wes leaned forward from the back. He was the most chill out of the three of them and typically played referee whenever Dion and Tyrone clashed. "I don't know, Dion. She seemed really pissed. If she's in town for a while, then she may not let us investigate."

Tyrone tapped the dashboard. "And you know we wanted Mrs. Montgomery's house as the example for the show."

Dion's shoulders tightened and he shifted in his seat. "The show is a big maybe and nothing to get our hopes up on. We might have to look somewhere else."

Tyrone faced him from the passenger seat. "Why? Mrs. Montgomery's house is one of the oldest in town.

If Mr. Montgomery isn't the spirit, it could be anyone. There's so much history and she's a local icon. She deserves to get recognized."

"I get that, but I doubt Vanessa would see it that way," Dion replied. His hands squeezed the steering wheel. "If she hears we're trying to film a pilot for an investigation show and want to use her grandmother's house, she'll doubt us even more. Just give it some time. She's a reporter, and we've given her a reason to check us out. Eventually she'll realize we're not trying to scam anyone. Especially Mrs. Montgomery."

Wes sighed and sat back. "I hope so. But the way she was shooting daggers with her eyes back there, I doubt it."

Tyrone reached over and patted Dion's shoulder. "Don't worry. Dion is on the case. If anyone can charm someone, it's our older brother."

Dion shrugged his shoulder so Tyrone's hand fell away. "I don't charm anyone. I just know how to get to what people really want." Seventeen years working in public service repairing roads and drainage issues for frustrated citizens had taught him to keep a level head and fix problems. "Vanessa is no different. I'll figure out what's holding her back and talk to her."

"Better you than me," Tyrone grumbled. "Honey is fine, but from the way she scowled, I bet she's evil and angry."

Wes shook his head. "You only say that because

you like smiling, pretty women who can't tell you're full of it."

Dion laughed and gave Wes a fist pound. "True that."

"Y'all just hating because the women love me," Tyrone said.

Dion didn't have to glance over to know his brother was grinning. The women did love Tyrone and his brother knew it. Dion used to envy his brother's easy ability with women. Dion had his fair share of relationships, but eventually they found his low-key, no-time-for-drama ways boring and moved on to the next, more interesting guy. Now that he was older, he'd come to accept that being the dependable guy wasn't always appreciated.

"If they love you so much, then charm Vanessa," Dion said.

"No way. She's all yours."

If only. A vision of her big bright eyes, full lips and even fuller breasts flashed in his brain. Dion shifted in his seat. Nope, not going there. She was from Atlanta, which meant she was more city than small-town girl. She worked in television, which meant she was probably high maintenance and craved attention. He'd had his world undone by a woman like her before. His only interest in Vanessa was convincing her that he and his brothers had her grandmother's best interests at heart. That was it.

Chapter Three

"We've got a tree down on Spring Street. Dion, can your guys handle it?"

A chorus of groans echoed in the cab of Dion's work truck. Though he didn't join in with the rest of his crew, the same frustration knotted his shoulders. The storm the night before hadn't been the worst they'd seen, but it had rushed through with enough wind and rain to bring down several trees and cut power to over three hundred homes.

Dion and his crew had spent the past twelve hours cutting trees to unblock roads, setting up cones to re-direct traffic away from flooded areas and calling in locations of other potential hazards. They were tired and more than ready to go home, relax and warm up. The overtime hours they'd get from working to recover from the storm damage would be welcome, but that didn't mean they weren't ready to get off after a long day.

He glanced at his three crew members and waved a hand to silence their collective groans. He was just as ready to get out of the cold and the wind. The exception was that Dion wanted to become the head of their streets division in the town's public works department, and refusing a request from the deputy director wouldn't help him achieve that goal.

"Did the tree just come down?" Dion asked. He was confident they'd handled everything out there.

"That last round of wind brought it down," his boss replied. Joe Evers was a former head of the animal control department who was best friends with the town manager and had worked that connection into becoming the deputy director of the department.

Everyone knew why Joe had gotten the job, but in the world of a small town, whom you knew mattered more than what you knew despite the anti-nepotism policies. Joe was the person selecting the next division manager; therefore, Dion was willing to do what was required to prove he was reliable and deserved his own promotion.

"Then we'll handle it," Dion said, ignoring the sighs and eye rolls of his crew.

"Great! I knew I could count on you, Dion," came Joe's overenthusiastic and relieved reply. "You and your guys are the best crew we've got. Don't worry about how long it takes. I've already approved the overtime. Come in when you can, and if you're hungry, use your credit card to cover dinner for everyone."

"Thanks, Joe. It's not needed, but we appreciate it. I'll call you when we're done removing the tree."

Dion hung up and suppressed a sigh. He looked at Bobby sitting in the passenger seat of his crew cab truck. Bobby was his second-in-command and though he wasn't against letting Dion know when he disagreed with a decision, he also tended to follow his lead.

"Come on, Dion," Bobby said. "We've been the main ones out here working every downed tree and power line since the storm came through. He could have given that tree to another crew."

"He gave it to us because he knows we're the best. It won't take long to handle this and afterward dinner is on me. Let's knock it out and be thankful for the overtime hours." Dion infused his voice with an optimism and energy he didn't feel.

"That's not even our area," Curtis Jones said from the back. He was the newest and youngest member of Dion's crew. "That's Phil's area. His crew should get the tree."

"The person who's assigned the job is the one who's supposed to get it," Dion said. "We were assigned the job, so that's what we're going to do."

"Man, I can't wait until you get promoted. We won't have to deal with this," Curtis grumbled.

"We don't know what'll happen with the promotion, so let's just focus on today." Dion's words shut down any further grumbling. They were paid to do a job and he was going to get it done. The people living on that road didn't care which crew was supposed to clear the tree. They only cared about having the road cleared. That's what he focused on as he pushed aside his frustration and headed in that direction.

An hour later Dion and his guys finished cutting up the large oak tree blocking the street and got the pieces moved to the side of the road. The rain started again in the middle of their work. Thankfully, not the soaking-wet rain they'd had the night before, but that didn't make the cold, misting rain that clung to their uniforms any less uncomfortable.

He used the radio to call in and let dispatch know the tree was handled. The dump truck would pick it up the next day. Thankfully, they didn't get another call to go out and handle another emergency.

Dion went to the back of the truck to secure his chain saw while his guys finished cleaning up the site. The sound of footsteps behind him preceded a woman's voice.

"Excuse me, sir."

Dion put the bed up on the truck and suppressed another sigh. He was ready to go home and wasn't in the mood to deal with a citizen asking a bunch of questions about what they were doing and why. Despite his annoyance, Dion centered himself. This was part of the job. He smiled and turned around. His eyes met the citizen in question and he froze.

Vanessa's big brown eyes widened as they met his. Dion's heart did a funky flip. His gaze dropped from her eyes to the tray in her hand and the four paper cups. The rich aroma of hot chocolate drifted to his nose. His stomach growled, reminding him lunch had been six hours ago.

"Oh... It's you," she said.

The surprise in her voice made his lips turn up. "It's me."

"I didn't know it was you," she said.

Dion pointed to the tray in her hands. "Does that mean you wouldn't have come with the tray?"

Her full lips lifted in a sheepish smile and one of her shoulders lifted. She didn't look as formidable as she had the afternoon before in her grandmother's driveway. A pair of dark gray leggings that clung to her shapely hips and thighs matched with a long mint green sweater and a black rain jacket.

"Maybe," she replied honestly. She glanced at his guys on the side of the road and then back to him. "You work for the town?"

Dion nodded and leaned an arm on the back of the truck. "For seventeen years. We got the call about a downed tree close to the end of our shift and came over to clear the road."

She shifted from one foot to the other. "That would have been me. The tree fell late this afternoon. I didn't think anyone would get out here to clear it so fast."

She sounded impressed. He knew her satisfaction wasn't with him personally, and he had no business feeling anything remotely positive about her satisfaction, but pride swelled in his chest anyway. He didn't overthink the feeling. Her good opinion might help her realize he and his brothers weren't out to take advantage of her grandmother.

"We try to get as many of the roads clear as possible. I wouldn't want anyone stuck in their homes or prevent emergency service vehicles from getting to a house if they need to."

She slowly lifted and lowered her chin. "When I was in Atlanta, we did a feature on the local public works department and the work they do. Before that, I never realized how much their work helped first responders do their jobs in an emergency. You all don't always get the credit." She lifted the tray. "Which is why I wanted to show some of my appreciation for your quick response."

Dion held up his hand. "There's no need for that. We don't do this work for gifts."

"I know that. But that doesn't mean I can't say thank you. I want to visit my grandmother later and thought I'd have to wait until tomorrow. Now I don't." She held out the tray. "I hope you like hot chocolate."

He did like hot chocolate. In fact, he loved hot chocolate. The sweet aroma drifted over to him. His stomach growled. Thankfully, the sound of the wind masked it.

He reached for one of the cups. "Thank you." He brought the cup to his lips. The drink tasted as good as it smelled. Better even. Rich, creamy and sweet. Dion was tempted to down the entire drink in a few gulps, but the way Vanessa's eyes were trained on him held him back. More specifically, the way her eyes were trained on his lips. A line formed between her brows and the tip of her tongue poked out of the side of her mouth.

Dion reached up with his hand to wipe the same corner of his mouth. She blinked and leaned back. Vanessa cleared her throat before her eyes met his.

"You're welcome," she said quickly. "It's the least I could do."

"You didn't have to do anything."

"After sitting inside watching you guys work, I couldn't help but do something. It's cold out here. Who knew you would be my knight in shining armor?"

Dion cocked his head to the side and gave her his I'm-here-to-serve smile. "Does this mean you're convinced I'm a good guy?"

Her eyes lost focus for a split second before she blinked and cleared her throat again. Her shoulders straightened. "The jury is still out on that. You cleared the road. It'll take more than that for you to clear the way to my trust."

"Don't worry, Vanessa, I'm more than willing to do what I need to earn your trust."

Something sparked in her eye. He would have

sworn it was interest, but before he could make anything of it, his crew members came over and interrupted them. Vanessa was all smiles and appreciation
as she passed the cups out among his guys, who
blushed and stuttered their own thank-yous in response. They were quickly smitten by Vanessa and
he couldn't blame them. Vanessa was the type of
woman to make a man forget the words in his head
with just a smile.

"Okay, fellas, we've got to get back to the camp,"
Dion said. "Let's load up the truck."

They grumbled but nodded and made their way
to the cab of the truck. Dion turned back to Vanessa
and held up his cup. "Thanks again for this."

She waved a hand. "It's no problem."

Their eyes met. Stuck for two breaths. Vanessa
blinked and glanced away.

Dion cleared his throat. He shifted from one foot
to the other. He had to keep this professional. He
couldn't let the hormones flooding his system like
the storm drains after the storm take him off track.

"I look forward to seeing you around, Vanessa,"
he said. "I'm going to prove to you that I'm a good
man." Ah, hell, why did he say that? It sounded way
flirtier than he'd intended.

Her lips parted into a cute O shape before her
brow rose. "Are you?"

He wasn't flirting with her. It didn't matter if his
heart rate increased and he felt a little twinge in his
midsection. He had to win Vanessa over for the sake

of his brothers and their interests. Not for anything else. She was only in town for a short time and a woman like her would want more than he could ever offer. He wasn't ambitious or exciting enough.

"I am. Only because I like your grandmother and I don't want to let her down." The light left her eyes a little, but that could just be a trick of the setting sun. "Have a good evening." He turned away and climbed into his truck before he got any more thoughts about a woman out of his league.

Chapter Four

Vanessa's eyes popped open at three in the morning. She sighed and stared up at the ceiling even though the room was so dark she could barely make out the edges of the ceiling fan. Waking up before the sun rose was an unfortunate side effect of being on a morning show for years. She had an inability to sleep in. Typically, that didn't bother her. Now she had way too much on her mind. Stuff she didn't want to focus on in the predawn hours.

Would she find another job? Why had she been dumped because of a horoscope? Why did her grandmother think her house was haunted? Why in the world had Dion Livingston's smile made her heart feel squishy?

She squeezed her eyes shut and groaned. Yeah, it was way too early for her to go through all of this. She tossed the covers back, knowing sleep wouldn't return, and jumped out of the bed. She showered and dressed before making a list of things to pick up at the grocery store later that morning. She had no idea what she would do for the rest of the day. Her grandmother had mentioned Tuesdays and Thursdays were the days she worked as a receptionist at city hall, so spending time with her was out of the question. Thanks to the storm and the downed tree, she'd spent all of Monday in the house cleaning things and watching movies where the guy didn't dump the girl because his horoscope said so.

After making coffee and sitting at the kitchen table with the radio playing a morning talk show, she picked up her cell phone and made the rounds through social media. Her former morning show colleagues would be in the studio, which meant they'd be on social media with updates and questions of the day. She shouldn't look at their accounts. It would only irritate her.

She looked and smiled at the question of the day: *When should kids be allowed to have a cell phone?* That had to be Gloria's question. She was always low-key trying to get parenting advice via the question of the day. That one would be hotly debated and generate a lot of discussion.

Her smile faded. She wouldn't be there to par-

ticipate in the debate or find out what had prompted
the question. Social media scrolling was a bad idea.

But since she was already torturing herself, she
might as well go all the way in. She clicked over
to Daniel's page before good sense could stop her.
The guy posted constantly. Mostly quotes, motiva-
tional phrases and pictures of him at various sport-
ing events for his sports podcast.

Daniel's page popped up and her heart froze. *Who
the hell is that chick?* She drew the phone closer to her
face. Daniel stood in the studio where they recorded
their show, along with his cohost, Craig. Between
them was a woman who looked at least ten years
younger than Vanessa. Young, pretty and wearing leggings beneath an oversize Atlanta Falcons jersey that
didn't hide the curves beneath. Her arms were around
Daniel's and Craig's waists and the guys draped their
arms over her shoulders. They all smiled, but the unknown woman leaned into Daniel's side.

Vanessa's eyes scanned the caption beneath the
picture. *"Great day in the studio with Falcons cheerleader Rebekah Rivers!"*

Okay, so she was a cheerleader they'd interviewed. Vanessa wasn't uninformed enough to think
professional cheerleading wasn't a sport. Daniel interviewed athletes from all types of sports. Including many female athletes.

But why was he hugging her, though?
Craig is hugging her, too.
The thought didn't ease her irritation. Rebekah

Rivers wasn't leaning into Craig's side. Craig's hand rested on Daniel's shoulder, whereas Daniel's hand cupped Rebekah's shoulder. Vanessa's eyes narrowed as she leaned in to get a closer look. Was Rebekah's hand gripping Daniel's shirt?

"Stop it, Vanessa!" She clicked the button to darken her phone screen.

Should you ever check an ex's social media account? That's what should be the morning show's question of the day. Though, she didn't need a poll to know the answer was a resounding hell no.

She glanced at the clock on the stove. It was four forty-five. Early enough to find coffee somewhere. Grabbing her wrist clutch and keys, Vanessa left the house. There was a Waffle House not too far from downtown. She'd loved going there with her mom and sister over the summers. So much so that she frequented the chain often after moving to Atlanta. The idea of a pecan waffle drenched in syrup with hash browns and crispy bacon eased some of the anxiety she'd felt sitting alone in her rental escape ward.

A few minutes later she pulled into the Waffle House parking lot. The yellow light from the sign reflected off four white trucks parked outside with the Sunshine Beach town logo emblazoned on the doors. Vanessa glanced through the large glass windows. Several people sat in one corner of the restaurant. All wore white shirts and dark blue pants like the ones she'd seen Dion and his crew in the day before.

Maybe Dion was one of the guys inside. Her heart

did a silly flip. The same silly flip it had done the day before when she'd seen him in all his masculine glory, standing on the side of her road, hauling chain saws and smiling as if the angels had gifted him with dimples for the sole purpose of blessing the human population.

She didn't know what visceral, hormone-fueled reaction she was having to the guy, but she didn't like it. Not just because he was probably scamming her grandmother, but because even though she and Daniel weren't together anymore, the sight of a cheerleader leaning into his side had irritated her. Meaning she could easily get snared in a rebound trap.

She scanned the workers through the window again. None of them looked like Dion, so she cut the engine and got out of the car. Even if he were there, she was going inside. Nothing was coming between her and a pecan waffle.

Vanessa went in and the mixed aroma of waffles, fried food and coffee greeted her. The two waitresses welcomed her and the cook at the grill lifted his spatula in greeting. Vanessa smiled and chose a booth on the opposite end of the restaurant than the group from the town.

A few minutes after she sat, one of the waitresses came over. She was a slim Black woman who looked about the same age as Vanessa with smooth dark skin, big bright eyes and long dark hair pulled back in a ponytail. The name pinned to her shirt was Sheri.

"You're in here early," Sheri said. She placed a napkin and utensils on the table in front of Vanessa.

Vanessa pulled the laminated menu out even though she didn't need to study it. "I'm used to getting up early."

"New in town?" Sheri asked.

"Just for a while."

"Have you been here before?"

Vanessa nodded. "Almost every summer when I was younger. My grandmother lives here."

Sheri's eyes lit up. "Oh really? Who's your grandmother? I grew up here and I know just about everyone."

Vanessa didn't mind Sheri's questions. Getting people to talk was part of her job as a reporter. People who already loved to talk and ask questions were typically easier to get information from. She needed to find out about Dion and his brothers. Maybe opening up to Sheri now would result in her providing information about the Livingston brothers later.

"Arletha Montgomery," Vanessa said.

Sheri's eyes narrowed and her head cocked to the side. She studied Vanessa for a second, before her jaw dropped and she straightened. "Oh my God! Vanessa?"

Vanessa blinked. "Yeah," she said slowly.

Sheri tapped her chest. "It's me. Lil Bit."

There was a moment of confusion, then memories flooded Vanessa's brain. Her eyes widened and she sat up. "Seriously?" She studied the woman's face more closely and recognized her.

The last summer she'd spent in the town she'd met Lil Bit at the skating rink. They were the same age, and they both had a humongous crush on a group of guys who'd also hung out at the skating rink. They'd formed an alliance with a few other girls to get noticed by the guys before the end of the summer. The rest of the summer was shenanigans resulting in Lil Bit ultimately getting the attention of the guy she'd liked and Vanessa eventually losing interest when her guy started dating someone else. She couldn't even remember any of their names.

She and Lil Bit had kept in touch over the next school year, and even through the following summer, but time had eroded that friendship. After Vanessa's father died, monthlong vacations in Sunshine Beach gave way to her grandparents visiting more to help her mom out.

"Yes, seriously," Sheri said. "Girl, I was just thinking about you the other week when I saw your grandma. She told me you're big-time in Atlanta and getting married to some guy on the radio. Congratulations."

The warm and fuzzy feeling she'd had seeing Lil Bit again faded. "Yeah, well, things change quickly."

The smile faded from Sheri's face. "Oh. My bad."

Vanessa waved her hand. "It's all good."

Sheri seemed to sense Vanessa wasn't in the mood to talk about the changes in her life. She grinned and pointed toward the coffee maker. "Hey, let me get you some coffee and let you look at the menu."

Vanessa slid the plastic menu back behind the condiments on the side of the table. "No need. I know what I want. Pecan waffle, hash browns smothered and covered, bacon and orange juice."

"I've got you." Sheri smiled, then turned and called out the order to the cook on the grill.

"Sheri," one of the guys on the other side of the restaurant called out. "Are you down there talking someone's ear off again?"

Sheri pursed her lips. "Mind your business, Leroy. I know her, thank you very much. Let me catch up with my friend."

The eyes of the men swung to Vanessa. Her cheeks burned from the sudden attention. Vanessa scanned their faces and confirmed none of them were Dion. She ignored the disappointment that tickled her chest.

"Introduce us," the same guy said, grinning at Vanessa.

Sheri shook her head. "How about you mind your business?"

The guys all laughed and went back to talking. Sheri winked at Vanessa before going over to make the glass of orange juice. A few minutes later Vanessa had several plates in front of her along with a steaming cup of coffee. She ate a huge forkful of the pecan waffle and groaned with pleasure.

"Good, huh?" Sheri said.

Vanessa nodded as she chewed, her mouth too full to attempt to reply.

"I should be sick of it since I work here, but I'm not." Sheri's eyes twinkled.

"How long have you worked here?" Vanessa asked after she'd swallowed.

"Oh, about a year. I moved back to town eighteen months ago after my mom got sick."

"Is she okay now?" Vanessa had vague memories of Sheri's mom. She'd let them have a sleepover one weekend and had picked them up from the skating rink a few times. She'd always been nice and hadn't ridiculed them for their ridiculous quest to gain the attention of the cool guys in the skating rink. Vanessa hoped she was doing well.

Sheri lifted a shoulder. "She's better, but the bills piled up. Your grandma comes by and checks on her, so that helps. Mom doesn't get out of the house as much, so company coming over gives her something to look forward to." Sheri snapped her fingers. "Oh yeah, did your grandmother get her house investigated?"

Vanessa's fork stopped halfway to her mouth. "You know about that?"

"Yeah. I told her about the Livingston brothers. They helped my auntie out when she had something going on in her house. They're good."

"They're scammers," Vanessa said.

Sheri's head jerked back as if she'd been slapped. "Scammers? Who?"

There was silence from the other end of the restaurant. Vanessa's eyes went from Sheri's shocked face to the sets of eyes trained on her with varying degrees of disbelief. Okay, so maybe she'd hit a nerve.

"Just to be clear, we're talking about the Livingston brothers who investigate ghosts, right?" Maybe she was mixing things up and had mistakenly insulted a reputable set of Livingstons in town.

"Yes, but they aren't scammers. They really do help people." Sheri's voice was convinced. She sounded as if Vanessa was foolish for even questioning the brothers' intentions.

"Yeah, helping people out of their hard-earned money."

Sheri crossed her arms. "No, ma'am, they really do help people, and it's not about the money. I'll admit, at first, I wasn't sure about what they were doing either, but then they found out what was going on at my aunt's place and gave her advice on how to make things better. She thought she needed to move, but her ghost isn't out to bother her. She's much more comfortable now. They've done that for a lot of people not just in town but all over the place."

There were several grumbles of agreement from the group across the restaurant. The other waitress and cook also nodded. Vanessa looked around with the practiced, neutral, I'm-not-judging-you face she'd had to learn as a reporter. Everyone seemed convinced Dion and his brothers were legit. For a second, she questioned herself. Then she remembered ghosts and hauntings weren't real.

"You wouldn't be saying this if you met them," Sheri said. "They're the nicest guys out there. Well… Tyrone is a wannabe player, but Dion and Wes are cool. Plus—"

"I met them on Sunday when I got in town."

Sheri's eyes widened. "And you still thought they were scammers?"

"Why wouldn't I? Some random guys show up at my grandmother's home to investigate a possible haunting?"

"Was Dion there?"

"He was the main one," Vanessa said. How could she forget him? He seemed honest enough, plus he'd helped her out with the tree the day before, but she still didn't believe in what he was selling. If anything, she wondered what had gotten him to take up this scam in the first place.

Sheri's brows drew together. "Dion wouldn't scam anyone. He's got a heart of gold and is the most decent guy I know. He took care of his brothers when his parents died."

Vanessa was intrigued. "Really?"

Sheri nodded vigorously. "Yeah. Turned down a scholarship to LSU and got a job to keep everyone together." Her eyes widened and she snapped. "Oh my God, he was one of the guys!"

"What guys?"

"One of the guys we crushed on that summer."

Vanessa coughed as the sip of coffee she'd taken went down the wrong way. No. There was no way. Not Dion Livingston. Sure she remembered one guy had a smile and dimples that made her thirteen-year-old heart flutter and melt, but he couldn't be the same guy.

"The guys you what?" a deep voice asked from the door.

Vanessa's entire body froze. She looked from Sheri to the door, where her gaze collided with Dion's. Hints of recognition knocked the remaining air from her lungs. Guess she knew why that smile made her feel all fuzzy inside. Dion Livingston was indeed one of the guys who'd made her teenage heart flutter all those years ago.

Chapter Five

Vanessa scrambled for something to say as Dion walked from the door to her table. He wore the same long-sleeved white shirt and blue pants uniform as the other workers in the restaurant. Unlike the others, Vanessa's eyes were attracted to the way the material stretched across his broad shoulders and wide chest, and she noticed how the blue pants were just fitted enough to draw her eye to the thickness of his thighs and the bulge right behind the zipper.

She jerked her gaze from his thighs and enticing crotch to his eyes. That wasn't much better. The corner of his full lips lifted as if he knew the direction her thoughts wanted to go. Dion was all man. Not a trace of the boy she'd noticed at thirteen. Thank goodness he hadn't noticed her back then. Talk about making an already awkward situation worse.

Dion stopped at the edge of her table and leaned one hand on the back of the seat across from her. "Who crushed on me?"

Vanessa waved a hand. "Nothing, Sheri was just telling me about how you helped her aunt.

His thick brows rose. "Oh really?"

Sheri chimed in. "We then started talking about that summer—"

"Apparently you've gotten a lot of people to buy into your game." Vanessa cut Sheri off.

Sheri's shoulders straightened. "I told you it's not a game. Dion and his brothers are legit."

The chorus of agreements came from the other end of the restaurant. Vanessa didn't care if she pissed off Dion's fan base, if she got the conversation moved away from her brief teenage infatuation.

"You're investigating me now, huh?" Dion asked, not sounding the least bit bothered to learn she'd asked about him.

Vanessa lifted a shoulder. "I'm a reporter. That's what we do." She cut another piece off her pecan waffle and took a bite.

Dion's eyes focused on her mouth as she chewed. She probably had syrup hanging from her lip. Heat prickled her cheeks, and she ran her tongue across her lower lip to remove anything hanging.

Dion cleared his throat and glanced at Sheri. "You're defending my honor?"

Sheri nodded. "You know it. Don't worry about Vanessa. She's naturally skeptical. I'm not surprised she became a reporter."

"You two know each other already?" Dion's voice held disbelief.

"Sure do. We hung out together one summer. Back then she didn't believe anything without seeing it for herself."

Dion's eyes shifted back to Vanessa. She tried to pretend as if his scrutiny didn't make her want to squirm. She focused on her food, but with his intense gaze on her, she was even more careful not to spill food on her shirt or stuff her mouth. And she really wanted to stuff her mouth. The waffle was damn delicious!

"You like to see stuff for yourself, huh?"

She glanced up at him. "I've learned not to take people at their word. Sometimes it's best to gather all information before making a decision."

"Oh really?" He sat down in the booth across from her.

One of the guys on the other end of the restaurant called out to Sheri for more coffee, and she quickly moved to refill their cup. Vanessa leaned back in her booth and eyed Dion.

"Who told you to sit down?"

"I've got an idea," he said.

"I'm not interested in any idea you have."

Damn, the man was big. He filled up the other side of the booth. She was used to being around good-looking men. Yet, here she was fighting hard not to drool over Dion as if she'd time traveled back to her teens.

"Hear me out," he said. "I think this will help both of us."

"In what way?"

"You like to see things for yourself to believe them. I respect that."

"So?" She took a bite of her hash browns.

"Why don't you come with me on a few investigations? See for yourself exactly what I do."

She put down her fork and crossed her arms. "Why would I do that? I already know there is no such thing as ghosts. Going with you on an investigation would just be a waste of both of our time."

He rested his forearms on the table and leaned forward. "So you telling me you've never once considered the possibility of ghosts being real?"

She rolled her eyes. "Yeah, when I was a kid and believed I could have a séance just to talk to dearly departed celebrities. But like most kids, I grew up and stopped believing in fantasies."

"What I do has nothing to do with fantasies or fairy tales. If you don't believe me, then come check it out. Don't just sit over there in your judgment, asking about me and my brothers with people in town. You really wanna know, put in the work."

Vanessa's chin lifted. He didn't raise his voice, but she heard the accusation. He didn't think she had what it took to get what she wanted. As if her unwillingness to go with him on an investigation meant she wouldn't do what's necessary to get to the bottom of something. His words struck too close to the reasons they'd fired her at the station. They also hadn't believed she could go the distance.

"I put in work," she snapped back.

"Then prove it."

"I don't have to prove anything to you. You're the one who wants something from me."

He shook his head. "No, I don't want anything from you. I'm trying to help your grandmother. You're the one holding her back from getting what she wants. And whether you do it now or wait until you leave, she will get what she wants. If you're really worried about her, then come with me and see what I do. If you still think I'm full of it afterward, then we'll go from there."

Dion parked his truck in front of Tyrone's modest ranch-style home. Grabbing the toolbox out of the metal case attached to his truck, he walked to the paved driveway down toward the house. Though the place was a rental, God forbid he step on Tyrone's perfectly manicured grass. He glanced over his shoulder just to make sure he hadn't inadvertently gotten the edge of the wheel of his truck on a single blade of grass on his brother's lawn.

Tyrone stopped lifting the front end of his car with the metal jack. "You didn't park on my grass, did you?" He called from the driveway.

When his brother called earlier that day asking for help changing the brakes on his car, Dion agreed to come over and oversee Tyrone's efforts. As the more mechanically inclined of the three, Dion used every request from one of his brothers to repair something as an opportunity to show them how to do it themselves.

Dion shook his head and laughed. "Just a little bit."

Tyrone ran around to the back of his car. "No you didn't! Man, I told you not to park on the grass."

Dion's grin widened when Tyrone saw not a hint of Dion's truck was parked on the lawn and scowled. "You sure get upset about your lawn."

Tyrone grunted. Instead of his normal fashionable attire, he'd listened to Dion and wore a pair of old jeans and a gray T-shirt. "I pay good money for my grass to look like that."

"You're obsessed, you know this," Dion said, reaching his brother.

"You know that your lawn is your calling card. People judge you by your house." Tyrone repeated the phrase their father had often used.

When Dion had given up college to look after his brothers, they'd all pitched in to make things work. Wesley picked up the cooking and baking while Tyrone, surprisingly, had taken over doing yardwork. Something he'd hated doing when their dad was alive. Tyrone was serious about making his home presentable, so Dion changed the subject.

He set down his toolbox and eyed the car. "You got the stuff I told you to get?"

Tyrone nodded. "Picked it up on my lunch break."

"Why are you changing the brakes on your car? Can't you just pay someone to do that for you, too?"

"They charge too much. Besides, why pay them when I know my big brother can handle it in no time." Tyrone grinned, revealing dimples similar to Dion's. He slapped his hand on Dion's shoulder.

Dion brushed his brother's hand away. "Nah, this is all you. I'm just here to supervise."

Tyrone scratched his jaw. "You were serious about that?"

"As a heart attack." He went into the garage and grabbed a folding chair that was propped against the wall. He set the chair next to the truck and plopped down. "Let's get started." Dion pointed to the wheels.

Tyrone looked from the car, to Dion, then back again. "You know I'm going to mess this up."

Dion shook his head. "You got it. I'll step in and help if I need to."

"Next time I'll just go to the auto shop," Tyrone grumbled as he went back to jacking up the car.

Dion chuckled. "It's not that hard."

"Says the man who can fix everything," Tyrone finished and rubbed his hands together. "Let's do this."

For the next two hours, Dion instructed his brother on how to change the brakes on his car. Dion only had to step in a few times. Tyrone might not think he was mechanically inclined, but he picked up on things quick.

"Bruh, I'm never doing that again," Tyrone said after they'd finished and gone inside to wash up.

"You know that wasn't that hard," Dion said. He pulled several paper towels off the rack and dried his hands.

"Not being hard doesn't make me want to do it again." Tyrone turned off the water and reached for the paper towels.

Dion laughed. "Fine, pay too much next time." He checked his watch. "I need to head home." It was nearly eight. He went to bed shortly after nine to get up early and have breakfast with some of the members of the various crews before going in.

Seeing Vanessa at Waffle House that morning had been surprising. A part of him wondered if she would be there again tomorrow morning. Another exceedingly small part of him hoped she would be. Only to further convince her to go on an investigation with him. Not because he'd enjoyed their back-and-forth that morning.

"It's still early," Tyrone said. "Have a beer before you go."

Dion shook his head. "You know I've got to get up early for work."

"Not as early as you get up. If you skipped breakfast at the Waffle House, you wouldn't have to get up so early."

"I like starting my day with my coworkers. It helps

me get my mind right before going in and dealing with the other bull." He ran a hand over his head and considered telling Tyrone about the invitation he'd extended to Vanessa.

"What's wrong?" Tyrone asked warily.

"Nothing's wrong."

Tyrone pointed at Dion. "Every time you rub your head like that you're trying to think about how to say something you know is going to piss people off. What is it?"

Dion dropped his hand. "I ran into Vanessa at the Waffle House this morning."

Tyrone's brows rose. "Really? What was she doing there?"

"Eating breakfast. She knows Sheri." Dion still couldn't believe that.

"Anyone who's friends with Sheri has got to be just as out of their mind as she is."

Dion shook his head and chuckled. "Sheri isn't out of her mind. She just doesn't like you."

"That was a year ago and she's still acting like it was yesterday. I told her I wasn't looking for anything serious."

Dion sighed and held up his hand. He wasn't in the mood to go down that road. "Whatever, man, apparently they knew each other from when Vanessa used to come to town as a kid. When I got there, she'd been asking Sheri about the ghost investigations."

Tyrone's eyes narrowed. "Hold up, she's snooping around on us?"

"What did you expect? She basically said she was going to look into us."

"I hope you cleared our names."

"I tried. She was back on her we're-scammers kick, but thankfully Sheri and the rest of the guys took up for us."

"Well, that's good. Did she agree to let us investigate Mrs. Montgomery's home after that?"

Dion shook his head. "Nah, she still doesn't believe us."

Tyrone's eyes narrowed. "If she keeps this up, you know she could ruin the television deal. Tiana is willing to come down and film what we do and present it to the network executives. We can't have Vanessa spreading rumors around town."

Tyrone worked full-time as an account manager at the radio station and moonlighted on the weekends event planning for parties and concerts the station hosted. His entertainment connections led him to meet Tiana, a producer at the Exploration Channel. Tyrone did what he did best and talked up their side hustle investigating ghosts. Dion still couldn't believe that quick intro had turned into the possibility of pitching what they did for fun as a television show.

"I know that. Which is why I invited Vanessa to go on an investigation with us." Dion spoke in a rush and tried to infuse optimism in his voice.

Tyrone stared at him for several seconds, blinked,

then turned away. He spun back around and pointed at Dion. "Tell me you're playing."

"Think about it. If we bring her along and she sees what we do, then she'll know we're for real."

"Or, she'll ruin the entire investigation by talking junk and telling the people we're trying to help that we're scammers."

"No, she won't." He'd have to make sure to bring up making fun of what they did wasn't allowed if she went with them.

"Did she say she'll go?"

"Not yet."

Tyrone let out a relieved sigh. "Good, that gives you time to take it back and tell her never mind."

"I'm not taking it back. This is the best way to convince her. You want to investigate Mrs. Montgomery's house, to do that then we'll need to get on Vanessa's good side. This is a good idea."

Tyrone shook his head. "I don't know. This seems like a bad idea. I don't think she'll take it seriously."

"She will."

"Then you take her," Tyrone said.

"Me?"

"Yeah, you. We've got a request from someone in Columbia. You can go ahead of me and Wes. Check things out and find out what's going on. We'll come up later and finish the investigation. By then you can show Vanessa enough of what we do to get her off our back, send her on her merry way, and we can move on."

Dion shook his head. "That's not what I asked her to do. I asked her to go on an investigation. That's all of us."

Tyrone lifted his chin and shook his head. "Nah, brother, this was your idea. Convince her to go with you to Columbia to check out this house and then get rid of her before we get there."

"Tyrone, come on, don't be like that."

"I'm gonna be like that. You asked her to go. You deal with her."

Chapter Six

Vanessa entered the sliding glass doors of the Sunshine Beach administration building thirty minutes before noon. She'd spent the past week exploring the town she'd roamed around during the summer as a kid. Many things had changed, but a lot of her familiar hangouts were still there, such as the skating rink where she and Lil Bit had spent every weekend her last summer in Sunshine Beach, the downtown drugstore with the best cherry colas ever and the park where there was always a pickup game of basketball going.

After spending the morning watching the various news programs, updating her résumé and making her own pecan waffles to avoid seeing Dion and his

Waffle House fan club, she'd opted to surprise her grandmother with a lunch invitation.

Arletha worked at the welcome desk in the middle of the first floor of the four-story building. Her grandmother's eyes widened, and she grinned as Vanessa strolled over to the desk. She had a phone to her ear and held up one finger. Vanessa leaned on the top of the desk and listened while her grandmother explained the process for paying for a pet license.

"What are you doing here?" Arletha asked after hanging up the phone.

"I was in the area and decided to drop by and see if you want to go to lunch with me." Vanessa grinned.

Her grandmother cringed. "Ooh. I just told Valeria and Donna I'd go with them to lunch."

"It's no big deal. I popped up on you," Vanessa said, trying to hide her disappointment. Her plans to rely on her grandmother to keep her company while she was in town were not going as expected.

Arletha waved a hand. "Don't worry about it. I'll call Donna and let her know my granddaughter is here. She'll understand."

Arletha reached for the phone. Vanessa placed her hand on her grandmother's forearm. "No, don't do that. I'll find something else to do. Besides, I can come by for dinner."

Her grandmother studied her. "Do you need something to do with yourself? I told you to take this time to rest and regroup. You don't have to fill every minute with activity."

Vanessa nodded. "I know. Believe me, I'm fine. I really thought to surprise you while I'm in the area. You don't have to worry about me."

Aretha shook her head. "No, I don't feel right just leaving you hanging. I can go to lunch with Valeria and Donna anytime."

"Grandma, seriously, don't change your plans for me. It's not a big deal."

A man walked up to the other side of the desk. "Hey, Mrs. Montgomery, how are you doing today?"

Vanessa's hand slipped off the desk. She quickly straightened herself, turned from her grandmother and met Dion's dark stare. Despite her plans to stay away from the Waffle House and avoid him, apparently fate had another idea. He looked good, as usual, in his uniform, his dimples on full panty-melting display as he smiled at her and her grandmother.

Arletha's face lit up. She swung her chair around to face him. "Dion, what are you doing here?"

Dion lifted one broad shoulder. "I had to drop something off in HR. Otherwise, you know I try to stay away from the main building."

Arletha chuckled. "Well, I'm glad I got to see you before leaving for my lunch break. You're always down at the public works site. I don't see you enough during the week. Things going okay down there?"

He nodded. "Same stuff, different day. But I can't complain."

"Complaining won't change things anyway. That's what Lou used to say." Her grandmother's smile turned wistful after mentioning her late husband.

"He was a smart man," Dion said. He glanced back at Vanessa. "Hey, Vanessa, how are you?"

The sound of her name on his lips turned her insides into warm honey. She straightened her shoulders and tried to ignore the feeling. "I'm fine, thank you."

"Vanessa came by to ask me to lunch," Arletha said.

Dion's brows rose. "That's cool. I won't hold you two up."

Arletha held out a hand. "You're fine. I'm going to lunch with Valeria and Donna. Why don't you take Vanessa to lunch?"

Vanessa sputtered for a second before gathering her thoughts. "Grandma, I don't need Dion to take me to lunch."

Arletha nodded. "I think you do. I know he invited you to go with him on an investigation. This will give you both a chance to talk about it."

"What? How…" Vanessa stammered.

"There ain't much that happens in this town that I don't hear about some kind of way," Arletha said with a grin.

Dion looked as if he was facing an oncoming eighteen-wheeler. "Mrs. Montgomery, it's okay. Vanessa can take her time to decide."

"No she can't," Arletha said. "Lou was knocking again last night. I know he's trying to tell me something, but I can't figure out what. The sooner Vanessa sees what you do, the sooner you boys can figure out what Lou wants. Besides, I know Tyrone has it all set up for you guys to film the investigation and pitch your show idea."

Vanessa blinked. "Show idea? What show idea?" Her suspicions rose.

"They boys are trying to get a television show about what they do. They want my house to be the one they use to pitch the idea."

"Only if you're comfortable," Dion said quickly.

"Of course I'm comfortable. I'd love to see you boys get your own television show. Another reason why you and Vanessa need to get things worked out."

The elevators opened and two women got out. "Arletha, are you ready?" one of the women called. Arletha glanced around the lobby. Her eyes lit up when she spotted another woman coming through the front of the building. She turned back to the women. "There's Francis to cover the desk for me. I'm ready."

The women walked over and stood next to Vanessa. Arletha grinned at them. "Ladies, this is my granddaughter Vanessa, I told you about. She's in town for a few weeks."

One of the women patted Vanessa's arm. "I heard about what happened. I'm sorry about the job. And your grandmother is right. You're better off without that guy."

Vanessa's cheeks burned. She tossed a glance at

Dion who, thankfully, looked away. She wasn't mad her grandmother told her friends the story. It wasn't as if it were a super secret. Anyone could find out that she no longer worked for the station, and Daniel already announced on his podcast that he was single. An announcement that earned him a ton of sympathy from his female fans.

"Um…thank you." Vanessa couldn't think of anything else to say.

Arletha came from around the back of the desk. "Donna, leave the poor girl alone. She knows all of that already."

"Is she joining us for lunch?" the other woman Vanessa assumed was Valeria asked.

Vanessa was ready to say yes, but her grandmother spoke first. "No, she's going to lunch with Dion. He's going to talk to her about the investigation he and his brothers are doing at my house."

Both women smiled and nodded as if the idea of a ghost investigation was the most normal thing in the world. Maybe it was normal in this town. She'd gotten the same reaction from everyone she'd spoken with. That and reassurance that Dion was the most outstanding, dependable and nicest guy she'd ever meet. She had to admit, all the admiration for Dion and his brothers had piqued her curiosity.

The next few minutes went by in a blur as her grandmother gave an update to Francis. Arletha and her two friends then ushered Vanessa and Dion out the front door and quickly took off for her grandmother's car parked toward the back of the parking lot. She and Dion were left standing in front of the building staring awkwardly at each other.

Dion spoke first. "I don't expect you to go to lunch with me."

"You want to use my grandmother's house to sell a television show?" She couldn't keep the disbelief out of her voice.

"My brothers do."

"You're working with them, so that means you want to as well."

He lifted a shoulder. A gesture she noticed he did a lot. "Personally, I think it's a long shot. I don't need recognition, but I'm not going to crush my brothers' dream."

"You really do believe you're helping people." There wasn't any mocking in her voice. She wanted to know why he believed ghosts were real and investigating them helped people.

His stance widened defensively, and he crossed thick arms across his chest. "I do help people. If you take me up on my offer, then you'll see for yourself."

Vanessa pulled her lower lip between her teeth. She'd originally declined because she didn't believe. She still didn't, but after a week of people asking her when the Livingston brothers were going to help her grandmother, she wanted to know more. If she wanted to prove they were scammers, then what better way than going for herself? Once she proved they were a hoax, then she could convince her grand-mother not to go through with this ridiculous plan.

"Fine. I'll come with you."

His eyes widened. "Really?"

"Yes. When is your next investigation?" She had to barely stop herself from rolling her eyes with the word *investigation*.

"This weekend. A family in Columbia called us."

"You don't just do this in Sunshine Beach?"

He shook his head. "We started out around here, but word spread. We travel a few times a month."

She hadn't expected that. "So a lot of people be-lieve this."

"Because it's true," he said with utmost confi-dence and a smile that made her blood heat up.

She reached into her purse and pulled out her wal-let. "You don't have to feel guilted into taking me to lunch." Plus, she needed more time to get over her juvenile response to his smile. She took a business card out of her wallet and held it out. "My cell num-ber is on here. Give me a call later and we can talk about the details for me going with you."

He took the card from her. "I'll call you tonight."

The edges of her mouth twitched. Damn her and the impulse to grin just because he said something super simple. "I'm having dinner with Grandma to-night. Just wait until later in the week."

His smile widened and his dimple deepened. "I'll do it however you like it, Vanessa."

And just like that images of him doing all kinds

of things to her just the way she like flashed in her head. Heat slid through her sex and her nipples tightened. Vanessa sucked in a breath and stepped back. "Good. I'll talk to you later." She spun on her heel and walked away before he noticed her reaction.

Chapter Seven

That evening, Vanessa and her grandmother settled in the leather recliners in Arletha's living room. Tray tables with steaming bowls of her grandmother's delicious chicken bog, a mixture of chicken, white rice and sausage, sat in front of them, and the local news played on the television. Her grandmother no longer used the formal dining room, and rarely ate at the table in the kitchen. Dinner in front of the television was her new routine.

"How was lunch with Dion?"

Vanessa's hand froze just as she was about to take a spoonful of food. "We didn't go to lunch." Vanessa didn't look at her grandmother, but she felt her stare.

"Why not? How are you going to realize Dion

and his brothers are good guys if you don't get to know him?"

"I don't have to go to lunch with Dion to get to know him. But don't worry. I've agreed to go with him on one of his investigations." She couldn't suppress the sarcasm in her voice.

Arletha patted the arm of her chair. "Good! You'll see for yourself."

Vanessa put her spoon down and faced her grandmother. "Do you really believe in ghosts? You honestly think Grandpa is haunting the house?"

Arletha ate a spoonful of chicken bog, then nodded. "Don't say it like that. I don't think he means any harm. I think he's just restless and can't settle."

"How long has this been going on?" Vanessa kept her voice neutral and started eating again. Any signs of judgment would upset her grandmother and she didn't want to do that. She needed to understand why her grandmother felt this way in the first place.

"I didn't really notice things until about three months after he passed. At first I thought I was just imagining him around because everything was new, and I missed him."

"What changed your mind?"

Arletha's eyes narrowed as she considered. "It was the little things. I'd wake up in the middle of the night and see a shadow at the foot of the bed. Instead of being afraid, I felt peaceful. Lou would never hurt me. Then came the knocks and moving small things around."

"Are you sure the house isn't settling or that you didn't move the items?"

Arletha pursed her lips. "I know what the house settling sounds like. Lou taps on things. Mostly upstairs in our bedroom, but sometimes he'll make noises in other areas of the house. He's also helpful," Arletha said with a surprised grin. "If I can't find something, I just ask him and eventually there will come a tap or creak from the room and voilà. There are my keys or the scissors or whatever else I can't find."

Vanessa didn't have a good rebuttal. She worried about her grandmother. Had being alone in the house for so long caused her grandmother's grief to manifest in this way?

"Maybe you should take a vacation or open the house to renters again."

"I know what you're thinking. You think I've lost my mind and I'm imagining things." Arletha chuckled. She didn't sound offended by Vanessa's assumption. "I thought the same thing for a while. Until I had a broken pipe and the plumber came by. He said a shadow hovered around him in the bathroom. He got creeped out and asked me if the place was haunted. Mind you, that's the first time in all the years we've rented this place that I've been asked that question."

"Really?" Vanessa said.

Arletha nodded. "The house has a lot of history, but before we moved in we had the grounds blessed and cleansed of evil spirits. We never had any trouble in all the years we were here. Now, three months after Lou passes, and suddenly I've got a ghost. It has to be him."

"What did you tell the plumber?"

"Exactly what I told you. That it's my late husband and he means no harm. That's when I decided to ask the boys to help me figure out what Lou wants."

Vanessa took a deep breath. She focused on eating while her grandmother's words sunk in. On the bright side, her grandmother wasn't afraid to sleep in her own home. She seemed comforted by the idea of her late husband keeping her company from the afterlife. If that were it, Vanessa wouldn't worry. The idea that she needed to spend money with Dion and his brothers to figure out what her grandfather wanted is what bothered Vanessa.

"Have you considered grief counseling?" Vanessa asked.

Arletha chuckled again. "I have already gone to grief counseling. We were married for forty-seven years. It wasn't easy to say goodbye."

Vanessa nodded. "I'm sorry. I'm just trying to understand."

"I know you're worried that this is all in my head. Even my counselor said maybe I'm imagining Lou is here out of guilt."

Vanessa choked on her spoonful of food. She coughed and slapped her chest. "What would you feel guilty about?"

Arletha held up her left hand. "I can't find my wedding ring."

"When did you lose it?" She'd noticed her grandmother's wedding ring was absent, but assumed she'd stopped wearing it because it was too painful a reminder.

Arletha rubbed her bare ring finger with her right hand. "About a month before he had the heart attack. It was kind of an ongoing joke between us. He'd ask me why I wasn't wearing it and I'd come up with some story about taking it off to wash my hands or put on lotion. He'd just smirk and say okay." Arletha's lips lifted in a wistful smile. Her eyes lost focus as if going back to those last days of playfulness with her husband. "He knew I couldn't find it, but he never gave me any grief about it. I have a habit of taking off rings and earrings around the house and forgetting where I left them. They always turn up. I was sure the same thing would happen with the ring, but..." Arletha sighed. "But he passed before I found it."

Vanessa reached over and placed her hand on her grandmother's forearm. "I'm sorry, Grandma."

Arletha waved a hand. "It's okay. I do feel a little guilty about not finding the ring, but not enough to make up what's happening around here." She sighed. "I just hope it turns up one day."

"I'll help you look for it." Vanessa was willing to turn over every piece of furniture in the house to find it if necessary.

Arletha smiled at her. "Thank you, but right now I'm more concerned about finding out why he's still here. I know you think the boys are a bunch of hacks, but they aren't. Let Dion show you what they do, and you'll see."

"I'll keep my mind open," she said rather than worry Arletha with her doubts.

"Thank you." Arletha shivered and ran her hands over her arms. "I'm a little chilly. Will you go upstairs and grab that sweater off my bed?"

"Sure," Vanessa said. She pushed her tray table aside and headed upstairs.

Arletha's lavender sweater was draped over the end of the bed. Vanessa crossed the room and picked up the sweater. The closet door creaked open just as she turned to walk out. Vanessa spun and faced the closet, then shook her head for being ridiculous. One talk with her grandmother and she was looking for signs that weren't there.

The back of her neck prickled. Her senses heightened as if she were being watched. Something moved in her peripheral vision. She spun again, but the shadow of the trees outside the bedroom window played across the floor. Vanessa put a hand to her heart and took a deep breath.

"You're being silly. Stop it." Still, she hurried out of the room. By the time she was back in the living room, she felt like a spooked cat.

"You okay?" Arletha asked as she reached for her sweater.

"I'm fine." Vanessa glanced at her grandmother and saw the smirk on her face. "What?"

"I thought maybe you felt your grandfather up there."

Vanessa narrowed her eyes. "Is that why you sent me to get the sweater?"

Arletha continued to smirk and slid on the sweater. "I really am chilly."

Vanessa didn't buy it. "No, I didn't sense anything." She sat and pulled the tray table back to her. "What are they talking about on the news?"

Arletha continued to smile but updated her on the expectations for a busy hurricane season. Vanessa focused on the television and the food. Her neck still tingled, but she refused to look around. There was no such thing as ghosts. She rubbed the back of her neck. She would prove all of this was nothing.

Chapter Eight

Dion stepped into the Waffle House for breakfast the next morning, and his gaze immediately zoned in on Vanessa. She sat in the same booth she'd been in the week before. Sheri talked while pouring coffee into Vanessa's mug. They both looked his way after he crossed the threshold. Sheri smiled at him and welcomed him in. Vanessa didn't smile, but her gaze held his.

Everything faded as she watched him. She studied him as if he were a riddle she didn't understand but wanted to figure out. Something else was in her eyes. Appreciation, maybe, or did he just want to see that? Just like he wanted her to understand him.

Wanted that look on her face to transform from confusion, to understanding, and maybe even yearning.

Vanessa bit the corner of her full lower lip as if he'd broadcast his thoughts. His pulse spiked and he jerked his gaze away. If he let his thoughts go where they wanted, everyone in the restaurant would know the way Vanessa affected him. He had to get himself in control. It was one thing to be attracted to Vanessa, but it was a whole bag of trouble to become infatuated with her.

"Good morning, Sheri." He threw up a hand. "Vanessa." He nodded and quickly looked in the general direction of her forehead before looking away. "I'll get my usual." He crossed over to the corner where his coworkers sat.

He'd call her tonight and make plans for the investigation. No need to talk to her in person. Not when he could barely make eye contact without his thoughts roaming to dangerous places.

He settled in on the edge of the booth and jumped into the conversation about the upcoming football games that weekend. Dion quickly defended his team when one of the other supervisors predicted a defeat that weekend. The conversation was almost enough to get his mind and attention off Vanessa sitting not far from them.

"Will you even get to watch the game?" Bobby asked. "I thought you were going up to Columbia this weekend."

Dion nodded and sipped his coffee. Sheri had placed the pecan waffle, eggs scrambled with cheese, and bacon in front of him and he'd already devoured most of that. "I'll DVR the game and watch it when I get back in town."

"You going on another investigation?" Susan, a member of a different crew, asked.

"Yeah, up in Columbia."

Susan's brows rose as if impressed. "You and your brothers are really making a name for yourself. You'll get that television show before you know it."

Dion just lifted a shoulder and took a bite of food. He didn't like talking about the show. No need to get excited about something that probably wouldn't happen.

Bobby slapped Dion on the back. "Once he gets it, then he'll up and leave us. He won't care about the division manager position."

Dion waved off Bobby's words. "I'm putting my hopes on that position more than getting the television show."

He preferred to focus on more realistic goals. After a heart attack took his dad when he was sixteen and lymphoma his mom three years later, he'd focused on making safe and logical decisions. All dreams of moving away from Sunshine Beach and living an exciting life in a big city dissipated when he chose to take care of Wes and Tyrone. Pinning his hopes on a steady paycheck and promotion made more sense than hoping for a television show.

"You've got this," Bobby said. "But if they don't give you the job, everyone here will complain."

Not wanting to think about a possibility of failure, Dion changed the subject. "Well, the only thing I'm focusing on for now is getting through today and the investigation this weekend."

"The investigation you're supposed to take me on?" Vanessa said from behind him.

Dion froze, then spun around. Vanessa watched him with a small smile on her full lips. The rest of his group fell silent, eyes wide and full of curiosity.

Gazes darted between him and Vanessa. Bobby spoke up first. "Hold up, you're going with him?"

Vanessa crossed her arms beneath her breasts and raised a brow. "Am I?"

Her hip cocked to the side. His eyes dipped to said hips before jerking back up to her face. She looked damn good in the burgundy leggings and a form-fitting gray thermal top.

He wiped his hands on one of the thin napkins before tossing it into the plate. "You are."

"Can we talk about that for a second?" She pointed toward her table.

A trace of irritation hung in her voice. Guilt twisted his stomach. He'd invited her two days ago and should have said something this morning, or at least called her the night before. Instead, he'd pro-crastinated because the sound of her voice turned his insides into mush.

Dion cleared his throat. "Sure." He stood and followed her back to her booth, ignoring the eyes of his colleagues focused on him.

"Where are we going?" she asked once they were settled into the seats.

"A couple in the Columbia area recently moved into a house and have had some unexplained things. They asked us to come and figure out what's going on."

"How long will the investigation take?" She leaned forward, resting her elbow on the table and propping her chin in her hand. Her breasts were also propped on the table.

Dion swallowed hard and turned to wave at Sheri. He made a drinking motion with his hands and she nodded. He needed something to focus on other than Vanessa and her curves.

"We usually spend the first day getting background info on the house and the land. We check for activity in the house at night." He accepted the cup of coffee Sheri dropped off with a nod. "If we can't finish up in a weekend we'll come back." He took his time adding sugar and cream while he spoke.

"Does it usually take multiple weekends?"

"It depends on each situation. Sometimes we figure things out quickly. Other times it takes a little longer. Spirits don't always want to participate."

"So, we'll have to stay overnight?"

"I'm staying overnight. You can drive up on Saturday morning." He spoke quickly.

She took a deep breath and leaned back. "No, I'll

go Friday. I don't want you waiting on me if traffic is weird. I talked to my grandmother and got a better idea of why she's doing this."

"You still don't believe her?" He could tell by the resigned tone of her voice.

"I believe she really thinks my granddad is in the house, but I also think that's because she's still grieving."

"You really think it's all in her head?"

She opened her mouth, then shut it. Her gaze slid away as she considered his words. Dion leaned onto the table. He'd seen that look before. The look of someone who saw or felt something they can't explain or didn't want to explain.

"Tell the truth," he said.

She glanced at him, blinked and sat up straighter. "It is all in her head. There's no such thing as ghosts, and despite what you or my grandmother may believe is happening there's always a logical explanation. I'm going with you to prove that."

He smiled, unbothered by the challenge in her voice. "Maybe I'll change your mind."

She scoffed, then picked up her coffee mug. "I doubt that." She took a sip and licked her lips.

Focus on the investigation, Dion. Not on her mouth.

"What do I get when I show you what we do isn't a hoax?" he asked.

She raised a brow. "*If* you prove anything all I'm offering is an apology and a handshake."

Her *you're-lucky-if-you-get-that* tone made him laugh. "I was hoping for something else."

"Something like what?" The corner of her lips kicked up and the hint of a tease filled her voice.

For the first time since sitting down, Dion made full eye contact. The connection sent a jolt down his spine. The way this woman hit so many of his *yes, please* buttons was ridiculous.

Dion leaned his forearms on the table. "Oh, I don't know, maybe that apology can be accompanied with an *Oh wise Dion, I'll never doubt you again.*"

Vanessa's jaw dropped, then she laughed. A full sexy laugh that made her eyes sparkle. His chest tightened as if someone squeezed his heart in a fist.

"I don't know about all that." She smirked at him over her coffee mug as she took another sip.

Oh, he really wanted her to figure him out. Believe him. Like him. "Let's wait and see, Vanessa. I'll prove that you'll never have a reason to doubt me."

Chapter Nine

Vanessa checked her watch as she got off the hotel elevator Friday evening. Half past seven and Dion still hadn't called to say he'd arrived. If he was playing a prank on her she was going to kill him. There was no way she'd let him or his brothers anywhere near her grandmother's home if he didn't show up.

She was halfway across the lobby on her way to the bar when the sliding glass doors to the hotel entrance opened and Dion crossed the threshold. She let out a sigh of relief. He hadn't ghosted her. Irritation quickly replaced the relief. Why tell her to be here by six if he wasn't going to show up until almost eight?

She marched toward him. "Where have you been?"

His glare stopped her short. He held up one hand. "Not right now, Vanessa."

She crossed her arms over her breasts. "I was here on time. You owe me an explanation."

"And I'll give you one if you give me a minute. I just pulled up. I need to check in. Can you at least let me get my room key and park my car before you go in?" His voice remained calm and steady even though his jaw and shoulders were tense.

She pursed her lips and returned his stare. A tiny part of her felt bad for jumping on him as soon as he'd walked through the door. But she had worried if he was showing up or not.

"You've got thirty minutes to meet me at the bar and explain," she said.

He looked to the sky and shook his head. "Fine. Thirty minutes." He walked past her without another look.

The man was fine, even when he was angry. That controlled restraint made her want to reach out and soothe him. She wondered what it would take to calm him down. Would the tension ease if she rubbed his shoulders? What if she massaged the back of his neck, then ran her hands over the smooth skin of his freshly shaved head?

"Stop it, Vanessa," she hissed to herself and cleared her mind of those thoughts. She was not here to figure out ways to make Dion relax. He needed to help her relax. She was the one anxious from wondering if he stood her up or ran into a ditch.

She went to the bar and ordered a gin and tonic along with lemon pepper wings. She was halfway through her wings when Dion joined her at the bar. He sat in the chair next to her and waved down the bartender.

"Let me get a rum and coke, please," he said, sounding as if he needed that rum and coke hours ago.

"Will that be all?" the bartender asked.

Dion glanced Vanessa's way. She paused in the middle of sucking seasoning off of her index finger. Dion's eyes darkened before they dropped to her plate. He turned back to the bartender.

"And an order of those wings. With blue cheese and a side of fries."

The bartender nodded. "I've got it."

Dion sighed and rubbed his temples. Vanessa picked up a napkin and wiped her hands. She'd planned to continue to give him a hard time about arriving late, but the slump in his shoulders combined with that sigh made her decide to take it easy on him.

"Long day?" she asked.

"Very long." He leaned his arms against the bar and stared up at the television.

"Want to talk about it?"

"Not really."

She nodded slowly and picked up another wing. "I just know that whenever I had a bad day at work it always helped to vent to a friend."

"I didn't realize you were my friend." The twinkle in his eye took the sting out of his words.

"Well, I'm the closest you've got right now," she said with a raised brow. "So spill it."

Dion chuckled and shook his head. The bartender came back with his rum and coke. Dion took a sip, then let out a long breath again.

"Just tell me what's up. If you don't want to consider me a friend, just consider it your explanation for getting here late."

The corner of his mouth lifted. He did have the sexiest lips she'd ever seen. "Are you always this pushy?"

"Answer that question yourself."

"Yes." He took another sip of his drink. "Just work. I tried to leave on time, but I couldn't."

"Let me guess, everyone and their momma wanted something from you before you left."

"Exactly. It's like they know I'm trying to leave early and suddenly need me for everything."

Vanessa turned sideways in her seat and faced him. "I've been there. It's the curse of leaving early. Any other day and everyone would ignore you."

"Ain't that the truth," Dion muttered.

"So what happened today to hold you up?"

"My boss caught me. We can't complete one of our projects until the cable company repairs their broken line. I told him that, but he'd promised a council member the work would be done today." He massaged his temple.

Vanessa's fingers twitched. She stopped herself before reaching up to rub his back. She was not supposed to touch Dion. She faced forward and picked up another wing instead. "What did you do?"

Dion's wings arrived and he immediately dug in. "I calmed him down, called the cable company. They'll be out tomorrow. I approved overtime for my crew to go out afterward."

"Sounds like you have things under control."

"I do, but it was his last comment that got to me." He ripped off a part of the wing he picked up.

He licked seasoning from his lips. Vanessa's gaze dropped to his mouth. Her body heated and she had to look away quickly. What had he been saying? Something about a comment.

"What comment?" She took a sip of her drink, hoping it would cool her down.

Dion darted a glance her way. He shifted in the chair before finally speaking. "He made an offhand comment about people not taking me seriously."

"Why would he say that? I saw how hard you and your coworkers worked to get that tree off the road. You resolved the problem with the project today, and everyone in town sings your praises. I don't see why anyone wouldn't take you seriously."

He sighed and wiped his fingers with a napkin. "My reason for leaving early is what led up to the comment."

Vanessa caught the hint. The ghost investigations. Despite her beliefs on his side hustle, she doubted Dion didn't care about the work he did for the city.

"That shouldn't matter. Your performance is what matters."

He scoffed. "Sometimes it doesn't matter how hard you work. People only see what they want to see." He took a long sip of his drink.

She sighed and pushed her plate away, his words stirring up feelings about her own situation. "I hear that."

He glanced her way. "Oh really?"

"Why do you think I came to South Carolina? I lost my job with the station because they didn't think I could fit in with their image of hard-hitting journalism."

"I don't believe that after you grilled me and my brothers about investigating your grandmother's home."

The surprise in his voice made her laugh. "Well, despite my persistence with you and your brothers, the people at the station didn't think I have what it takes to fit their new vision."

His eyes met hers. "You don't seem like the type of person defined by other people's opinions or expectations. Forget the people at that station. You'll find something better." He spoke with a confidence in her abilities she didn't feel. A confidence she needed right now.

She turned back to her drink and drummed her nails on the glass. "I hope so."

"You will. Believe me."

She cocked her head and smiled at him. "You're

very confident about something even I'm not sure about."

"You put off that kicking-ass-and-taking-names vibe," he said, waving a hand in her direction. "I get the feeling you'll rise up and show your haters why they never should have underestimated you in the first place."

She narrowed her eyes. "You really think all of that when you see me?"

So many people looked at her and made a different assumption. As if her bra size prevented her brain from functioning. She'd refused to let other people's assumptions make her hide her figure under oversize or unflattering clothing. She liked her body and wore figure-flattering clothes. Not once had Dion looked at her as if all he saw was her breasts and behind. If anything, he made a point not to ogle her.

Dion's eyes didn't drop from hers. "I see all that and more."

Heat spread through Vanessa's midsection. "I don't get the ghost thing, but in the short time I've been in town I can tell people shouldn't underestimate you."

He looked surprised. "How?"

"Everyone sings your praises. Not just the work you do, but how you stepped in to take care of your brothers."

He glanced away quickly and waved off her words. "I did what I had to do."

"Did you really give up a scholarship to raise them?"

"It's not that big of a deal. Wesley was fifteen and Tyrone was thirteen when my parents died. They were self-sufficient. I stayed home because I wanted keep us together." He spoke the words briskly as if reciting a memorized speech he was tired of delivering.

"Would you have been split up?"

"We have an aunt in DC who wanted us to move there, but after Mom and Dad died within three years of each other, moving was too much too soon. We don't have family here, but we have friends and people like your grandparents who cared about us. Wes was always good in school, but Tyrone needed a little more guidance."

She cocked a brow. "I can see that."

That loosened the stiffness around his mouth and he cracked a half smile. "He listens to me. If we would've moved to DC, he wouldn't listen to my aunt and might have made bad decisions."

"You became dad and brother."

He shook his head. "I'll never fill my dad's shoes. I just tried to give them both stability. People say I raised them, but they helped give me something to focus on other than my loss."

"You're admirable and strong. Forget your boss. I believe he's underestimated you, just like my bosses underestimated me."

He glanced her way and a moment of respect

passed between them. The urge hit her to reach out and rub his back and hug him for the boy he'd been who'd had to grow quickly into the dependable man he'd become. The slightly embarrassed look that filled his eyes when she first praised him gave way to a glimmer of gratitude. He leaned slightly forward. Vanessa inched toward him in return. Someone laughed at the end of the bar.

She glanced away and waved down the bartender. "Check, please." She needed to leave before she started feeling all warm and silky inside.

"I'll take mine, too," Dion said.

She looked at his plate. "You're not done."

"I'm tired. I'll take the food to my room. I just want to take a shower and get in bed."

A picture of Dion in the shower filled her mind. She cleared her throat and rubbed the back of her neck. "Yeah. I think I'll crash, too."

They cleared their tabs. The bartender brought Dion his to-go box, and they walked together to the elevator.

"What floor?" he asked.

"Fifth," she said.

"Me, too."

Did he sound excited about that? Bigger question: Why had her pulse increased? They exchanged glances, smiled, then glanced away. The elevator doors opened before Vanessa could think of something to say.

They rode up in silence, each beep of the elevator adding an additional electric hum to the air. She hoped he was going in the opposite direction of the hall than she was. He did not. They both turned left once they reached their floor.

She stopped in front of her door. Dion stopped with her.

"This is me." Her voice sounded husky. She cleared her throat and tried to ignore the pulse rushing in her ears. "Thanks for walking me to the door."

He pointed to the door across from hers. "This is me. I guess we're neighbors."

Heaven help her he was across the hall. She swallowed hard. "I guess so."

He reached over and touched her hair. Vanessa sucked in a breath as his fingers slid through her hair. His fingers didn't touch her skin, but the heat of his body singed her. The spicy scent of his cologne enticed her.

He pulled back with a white piece of lint between his fingers. "You had something in your hair." The deep rumble of his voice vibrated across her skin.

"Oh. I thought you were trying to flirt with me."

His lips lifted in a sexy smile. "You'll know when I'm trying to flirt with you." He gave her one last heated look before he turned to his door.

"You'll know when I'm trying to flirt with you."
He couldn't believe he'd said that. Had to have been the rum and coke. That's what he told himself the following morning. There was no other reason

why he would have opened the door to flirtation with Vanessa. That door needed to remain closed. Locked. Bolted shut. He'd just gotten caught up in their talk the night before. She'd listened and related to his frustration at work. She'd praised him like everyone else did for what he'd done at nineteen. That was all. No big deal.

But why did he like hearing it from her, though?

The way she talked about wanting to prove her old bosses wrong meant she'd return to Atlanta or someplace bigger and start her career in front of the camera again. Which meant not staying in Sunshine Beach. Not starting something with a guy who fixed potholes every day.

"You're a great guy, Dion, but I deserve more. I can't spend my life with a blue-collar worker."

Three years had passed, but those words still got to him. He'd tried to convince himself his ex-girlfriend Keisha was conceited, but the women he'd dated since had broken things off for a variation of the same reasons.

"We don't go out enough." When he spent weekends ghost investigating with his brothers.

"Why do you always go to bed so early?" When he turned the lights off at 9:00 p.m. because he had to go to work early the next morning.

"Good sex isn't enough. I need a guy to pamper me." When he'd refused to pay for a damn Birkin bag.

He'd learned the hard way. He was good for a short-term, no-expectations relationship, but he wasn't what women wanted long term. Nice-guy dependability wasn't enough to make up for the charisma he apparently lacked.

Too bad he was attracted to the wrong women. Tyrone told him plenty of times to quit messing around with high-maintenance women.

Someone knocked on his hotel room door. Dion was dressed and ready to make his way to the Richardsons', the couple who'd hired them for the investigation. He glanced out the peephole. Vanessa stood on the other side.

He swung open the door and his body forgot all the reasons his brain said not to flirt with Vanessa. Her thick hair hung loose around her shoulders. The off-white scooped-neck sweater she wore gave an enticing glimpse of smooth honey brown skin while her fitted jeans dared him not to notice her full hips and ass.

She raised a brow when he just stared. "Are you ready?"

Dion blinked and shifted his weight to one foot. "Yeah, I'm ready. I was just about to call you."

Her smile should be declared a threat to the male heart the way it personally attacked his. "Let's go. Can I ride with you instead of driving?"

"Yeah. I'm in my truck."

"That's fine. I don't have anything against trucks," she said in a teasing voice.

"Okay… Well, let's go." He grabbed his keys and they headed for the elevators.

They didn't talk as they left the hotel. Thankfully, there were other people on the elevator to avoid the awkward-as-hell tension that had ridden up with them the night before. As soon as the doors closed them in the cab of his truck, the smell of peaches drifted to his nostrils. He breathed in deep.

"What's that smell?" he said as he pressed the button to start the engine.

"What smell?" Vanessa scrunched up her nose and glanced around.

"It smells like peaches or something."

"Oh." She let out a hesitant laugh. "That's my lotion. Sorry, I didn't think about allergies. Does it bother you?"

No, it didn't. He loved peaches. A ripe peach on a summer day was one of the best things in life. Her smelling just like a peach made his mouth water for a taste. Made him yearn to explore every nook and cranny from her neck to her navel, and below to see if she smelled, no tasted, just as sweet.

He jerked the truck in gear. "It's strong."

"Oh…my bad. I won't wear it again around you."

"You don't have to change what you wear. We won't be around each other a lot."

"Does that mean you're giving up investigating my grandmother's home? Because if you plan to change my mind, then you'll have to be around me."

"I haven't given up. I just mean we won't be in cars and close to each other." In cars where he'd be distracted by how good she smelled.

A few minutes later, she asked, "How did you and your brothers get started with this stuff anyway?"

He relaxed. He was more comfortable talking about that. "Our grandmother used to tell us ghost stories. At first we thought she made them up, but as we got older we realized she was talking about places around town. Some of the stories she told were about experiences from members of our family. One day we decided to spend the night at one of the old houses she said was haunted. It's called the Bookersville place."

Vanessa pressed a hand to her chest. "Wait, so you willingly spent the night in a house that was supposed to be haunted?"

"You sound like you wouldn't do that."

"I wouldn't."

"I thought you didn't believe in ghosts."

She rolled her eyes. "I don't but that doesn't mean I like to tempt fate. Rickety old houses probably have all types of building code deficiencies. Not to mention creepy crawlers of the four- and eight-legged kind." She shivered.

Dion laughed. "True. There were spiders and probably mice. In fact, that's what we originally thought we heard making noise in the house. But something else was going on. You can feel a spirit when it's there."

"What does it feel like?"

Her voice had a neutral, I'm-not-judging-you quality to it, but from the way her eyes narrowed, he couldn't tell if she really wasn't judging him or if she was thinking he was full of crap.

"It's hard to explain. It's like static electricity. All over your skin. If they're close enough you get chills. The air feels colder. Wesley is more in tune to the type of energy. Sometimes he can tell if the spirit is angry, sad or simply curious." He glanced at her.

"Hmm…interesting." She nodded. "You and Tyrone can't feel that?"

Maybe inviting her along wasn't such a bad idea. She was listening and hadn't thrown a judgmental look his way. Maybe she was starting to believe him.

"We can sense activity. Most people can but choose to ignore the signs. We were in tune enough to know the noises we heard that night wasn't just rustling. We felt as if someone was in the room with us."

"And you didn't leave?"

"No, stayed the entire night. It was the scariest thing we'd ever done, but when we made it through the night we wanted to know more. So we checked out Grandma's story. She said the house was haunted by a man whose wife killed him years ago. We searched the records, and that story was true. So we started checking out the stories of other places and fact-checking the records. Before long, the thing we were doing out of curiosity became a full-time side hustle."

"And people actually pay you to check this out for them?"

"They do. We started doing investigations for

free. Tyrone decided we were spending too much time researching without asking for some type of compensation. We don't charge a lot, and we still help some people for free if we know they can't afford anything."

"What does my grandma fall into?"

The question he'd been waiting for. "We aren't charging her. All we want is the ability to film what we do in her home."

"For the pilot?" An "aha" tone entered her voice as if she'd found the real reason.

"Tyrone wants to get on television. TV is his dream. He's got hookups through a producer at the Exploration Channel. They feature paranormal investigation shows. When they heard about three Black guys investigating ghosts, she said they would be interested."

"Hmm…interesting."

He glanced in her direction. "What does that mean?"

She gave him an innocent look. "It just means that's interesting. I'm here to observe and that's what I'm doing."

He wanted to know if that was just her go-to I-don't-know-what-else-to-say phrase or if she really was interested. He decided not to push it. They were taking baby steps. Dion hoped he'd made some headway with their conversation. She'd listened without a snide comment, so that was a good thing. She wasn't outright calling him a scammer anymore.

They arrived at the location a short time later. The Richardsons were a young white couple, newly married, who'd moved to Columbia from Ohio for the wife's new job and had purchased the first house they could find in the southeast part of town. Charles Richardson was Dion's height, thin as a reed with curly brown hair and friendly eyes. His wife, Kara, was almost as tall as her husband, just as thin but with straight red hair. They both enthusiastically greeted Dion and Vanessa before inviting them in the house.

"Why don't you tell me what's going on," Dion said once they were settled around the dining room.

Kara glanced at Charles. He nodded and she turned back to Dion. "We noticed it right after we moved in. We got such a good deal on the house we didn't think about asking for more background. We knew it was a fixer-upper, but that's what we wanted. Something vintage, ya know."

Dion nodded. "How old is the home?"

"It was built in nineteen eighty-five. We don't know much about the previous owners or the land."

"Wait, so you moved all the way to South Carolina from Ohio and didn't bother to look into the house you purchased?" Vanessa asked. She used her calm reporter's voice, but the judgment still rang through.

Kara and Charles both shifted in their seats before

Kara answered. "We had to move quick. I didn't have a lot of time before starting my new job."

"And we both wanted to be in a more rural area," Charles chimed in.

Dion nudged Vanessa's foot with his. She glanced his way and he smiled, but hoped she noticed the be-quiet look in his eye. This was his investigation, not hers.

"Don't worry, my brothers and I will check out the history of the house and the land," he said. "Tell me about the strange things."

"Well, I keep seeing shadows," Kara said. "Mostly in the bedroom and upstairs bathroom. Typically, when Charles isn't home."

Dion glanced at Charles. "Have you seen anything?"

Charles shook his head. "I haven't, but sometimes I feel like someone is watching me. At night at the foot of the bed. When I wake up no one is there."

"I've felt that, too," Kara said. "When I get up at night to go to the bathroom I see the shadow. He only shows himself when I'm alone."

"Your ghost is a misogynistic Peeping Tom?" Vanessa asked with a shake of her head.

Kara's cheeks turned red. Charles reached out and took her hand. "It bothers me because I'm not there to protect her when strange things happen."

"What are you going to do against a ghost?" Vanessa asked.

Dion kicked her foot a little harder this time. She

glared at him and he stared back. She took a deep breath and gave him a *fine* expression.

He turned back to the Richardsons. "This isn't the first time we've heard of a spirit only bothering one or two members of a family."

Kara nodded and leaned forward. "What do you do next?"

"I'm going to do a little digging into the history of the house and the land. My brothers and I will come back this afternoon and we'll start our investigation tonight. If you don't mind, we'll spend the night here to see if we notice anything."

Charles quickly agreed. "That's fine. Thank you so much."

They wrapped up and Dion and Vanessa left. In the car, Vanessa shook her head. "Can you believe that? A ghost who only shows up in the bathroom."

He glared at her. "What I can't believe is the way you completely undermined them back there. They're genuinely concerned, and they don't need your snide remarks."

"I wasn't snide. I was intentionally neutral."

"No you weren't. You were snide and judgmental. I brought you here so you could see what we do. Not insult my clients. If you can't do that, then you can just drive back to Sunshine Beach today."

Chapter Ten

"I'll drop you off at the hotel."

Vanessa stared at Dion's stoic profile. She hadn't meant to come across as judgmental. She'd only wanted to understand why two adults believed a ghost was in their house. Maybe some of her skepticism had come out in her voice, but it wasn't intentional. Her mind still tried to comprehend what the Richardsons said was happening in their home.

"What are you going to do?" she asked.

"I've got an appointment with an archivist at the library." His answer was quick and efficient. As if she should've guessed he was visiting with an archivist.

"Take me with you."

He shook his head before the words were out of her mouth. "No. You can go back to Sunshine Beach."

"I don't want to go back."

"Then what do you want, because it's obviously not to sit back and observe what we do," he said in a clipped tone.

"I do want to observe." As farfetched as their story was, she was intrigued. Vanessa wanted to believe it was their imagination, but the real worry in their voices interested her.

"Observing doesn't include throwing out unnecessary comments aimed at undermining me or making my client feel uncomfortable." He held up a hand. "You know what. Don't worry about it. I'll just take you back to the hotel."

Her hand shot out and clasped his bicep. "No, don't." His arm was rigid and rock hard beneath her hand. She had the urge to squeeze, run her hand farther up to his shoulder. Find out if the rest of him was just as solid.

Dion looked down at her. She snatched her hand back. Her heart sprinted as if she'd just been caught touching something she shouldn't but wanted to touch again. She took a long, steadying breath.

"You're right," she said. "I shouldn't have let my doubts come through when I spoke with them. It was rude and unfair to you and them. I'm sorry."

He glanced at her from the corner of his eye. "Apology accepted."

He sounded reluctant to accept. "You sure?"

"I'm sure. Let's just move on. I'll drop you off at the hotel and we can talk about your grandmother's place later."

"No, I'm serious. I want to go with you. I promise I will just observe. I'll hold my questions until later when you can roll your eyes all you want."

"I don't roll my eyes," he said in an affronted voice.

"Your eyes may not roll, but your voice implies the action."

The corner of his lip lifted. "My voice?"

"Your voice channels Barry White when you're frustrated," she teased, referring to the late great, soul performer who sang seductive love songs in a smooth baritone.

"Channeling Barry White?" he said with a disbelieving laugh. "I don't channel Barry White."

"Oh please, don't act like you don't know your voice was made for late-night phone sex." Vanessa snapped her mouth closed the second the words left. Embarrassment heated her neck and face.

Dion's low rumble of a laugh filled the cab. Full and deep and, yes, made for late-night phone sex.

"That's a first," he said. "Fine, I'll take you to the library." He glanced at his watch. "I don't want to be late. Just remember you promised to just observe."

She grinned and relaxed. "Thank you." She was also thankful he wasn't going to press her on the comments about his voice. She was not going to flirt with or do anything with Dion not related to finding out the truth behind his investigations.

The more time she spent with him, the less she believed he'd targeted her grandmother. Dion was turning out to be the nice guy everyone said he was. She glanced at him out of the corner of her eye. Was he single? A guy like him, handsome, gainfully employed, seemingly kind, had to have someone special at home.

As much as she wanted to ask, she kept the thought to herself. She wasn't on the lookout to date another superstitious guy, and she wasn't into quick flings. Which was all anything with Dion could be because she planned to eventually leave Sunshine Beach. Until then, she'd be better served keeping all thoughts of Dion and his bedroom voice out of her head.

"Damn... I bet that's our spirit."

Vanessa glanced up from her phone to Dion sitting in the chair across from her. They'd arrived at the library where the archivist, a nice older woman with an obvious enthusiasm for history, had quickly shown Dion where the digital records were kept. He'd spent an hour researching the history of the various people who owned the property going back before the current home was built in 1985, and then spent another hour combing through old newspaper articles to find out if there were any interesting stories reported at the location.

Vanessa could honestly say she was bored out of her mind. While she loved investigating a story and reporting the news, combing files for an unknown clue to a dubious mystery wasn't the type of research she enjoyed. To his credit, Dion seemed to really get into digging through the materials.

She slid her phone into the back pocket of her pants and leaned forward. "What did you find?"

They were in a small room where the library kept its microfiche and digital records. No one else was in there with them. Guess some people had more exciting plans for a Saturday than searching archives.

"I think I found the person haunting the Richardsons." Excitement filled his voice.

"Who is it?"

"The history of where the house is located is interesting. Back in the late 1800s there was a railroad stop in a town called Kingsville. Floods eventually destroyed the town. Much of the town's history was lost except for a few locals who try to keep the memory alive. A school and church were on that property. The land's been subdivided, but if I'm right..."

He turned to his laptop on the table next to the microfiche machine. A map of the area was pulled up on the screen. "Based on the GIS map, this is the same area."

"There really was a town there?"

He nodded. "Apparently." He pointed to the screen of the microfiche machine. "It's a small article, but a kid died on the property."

Vanessa gasped. "No."

"Yeah." Dion scanned the article. "It was during a

tent revival at the church. A fire broke out, believed to have been intentional. The last thing witnesses remember is the child looking for his mom. He was trampled in the rush of people trying to get out."

Vanessa slid closer to Dion so she could read the article herself. "That's terrible." Her heart ached at the idea of a child losing their life in such a terrible way.

"His mother found his body the next day." Sadness filled Dion's voice. "After the fire the church and school weren't rebuilt. A flood came through the next year and people moved away. There's an article from 1960 about the ghost of a kid haunting the property. The article didn't have the full story, but mentioned legends passed down by the people who still live in the area about the ghost of a child searching for his mother. It was a Halloween article chronicling various ghost stories in and around the city. They didn't do any research into the legend."

"You think the ghost of this kid is what's at the Richardsons' home?"

"I do. The house was built in 1985, but the owner sold the place a year later. It's changed hands multiple times since then. Until it became a rental property in the early 2000s."

"I wonder if the renters noticed anything, too."

Dion shook his head. "I'll ask Tyrone to look into that. He's good at getting information out of people. He can track down a previous owner and see if they experienced something similar."

Vanessa glanced back at the screen. "Would that be why the ghost is following Kara? He's looking for his mother?"

Dion lifted one shoulder. "Possibly. We'll have to ask."

She sat up straight. "How are you going to ask?"

The sparkle in his eye when he glanced at her made her stomach flip. "That's the fun part you'll see tonight."

A spark of anticipation flared in her chest. She wasn't really buying into this. The story of the child was tragic, but that was over a hundred years ago. There was no way the ghost of a child was really sticking around all these years later. She was getting caught up in Dion's beliefs. Hard not to do when he was so cute as he chased the lead. Cute and focused.

"You're going to let me go back tonight?"

"You kept your promise and didn't complain while I went down this rabbit hole. You even look like you want to know the answer."

She scoffed and pushed his shoulder. "I'm curious, but I still don't believe in ghosts."

He only smiled at her denial. "Still, you're interested. That's how it always starts."

Chapter Eleven

Dion met the disbelieving eyes of Tyrone and Wes. The trio stood in Dion's hotel room. He'd given them a quick rundown of what he'd learned from the Richardsons and his research of their property. They both were eager to get back and try to detect any activity. That was until he'd spoken his last words.

Wes recovered first. He blinked, placed one hand on his hip and pointed the other at Dion. "You told her she could come?"

Dion nodded and straightened his shoulders. He would not squirm under his brothers' scrutiny. "I did."

Tyrone shook his head. "I don't like it."

"Why not?" Dion asked.

Tyrone's eyes widened and he looked at Dion as if he'd lost his mind. "Why not? Because the woman thinks we're frauds. You said yourself she was snarky during the visit with the Richardsons. Why bring her back and possibly make things worse?"

"Because she's curious. I'm not saying she's convinced, but she's interested enough to want to stay involved. Once she sees this through, then she's more likely to let us investigate her grandmother's home."

Tyrone sucked his teeth. "I don't know, bruh."

"Come on, you know me. You know I wouldn't agree to this if I didn't think it would help."

"Maybe," Tyrone said. "But I saw you two when you got back to the hotel. All grinning and giggling up in each other's faces."

Wesley nodded. "There was a lot of grinning and giggling."

Dion waved off his brother's comments. "Nobody was doing anything like that. I'm trying to get on her good side. That's all."

"You telling me nothing happened between you two?" Tyrone asked with a raised brow.

"Everyone ain't like you. Just because I was at a hotel with a woman doesn't mean we're going to end up in bed."

Wesley chuckled and sat on the end of the bed. "He's got you on that, Tyrone."

Tyrone pulled on the edge of his shirt. "Whatever."

"As much as you don't like it, you know this is a

good idea. You want to investigate Mrs. Montgomery's house more than all of us because it's your dream to take this to television."

"It's not just my dream. It's our dream." Tyrone motioned his hand among the three of them.

"No. It's your dream. I support it, but you want this."

Tyrone's chest puffed up. "You know what, that's your problem. You're afraid to dream big. You need to get over that. Stop settling and believe in something bigger."

Dion stepped to his brother. "Don't go there, Tyrone."

"I'm going there. You're trying to act like you don't want this television deal just as much as us because you're scared. Just admit it. You want us to succeed a hell of a lot more than you want to continue patching potholes."

"That's the real problem. You don't respect what I do."

"I respect the hell out of what you do. You think I don't know your work put me and Wes through college? What I don't respect is you believing that you can't do more."

Wesley jumped up from the bed and stood between the two. "Hey, hey, calm down. Both of y'all. Neither of you need to go there, alright. We all want this to do well. What's most important right now is helping the Richardsons, getting Vanessa to chill and then helping Mrs. Montgomery."

Dion glared at Tyrone for a few seconds before

nodding. "You're right. Let's just do what we've got to do for now."

Tyrone turned his head away before saying, "Cool with me."

Wes nodded and slapped their chests. "Good." He stepped back. "Now hug it out."

Dion and Tyrone both turned to him. "What?" they said simultaneously.

Wes shook his head and pointed between the two of them. "You heard me. Hug it out. We already have an investigation tonight. We don't need to bring any negative energy with us. Go ahead. Hug it out."

Tyrone shook his head. Dion rolled his eyes. Vanessa was right. He did have that ability. He let out a soft chuckle.

Tyrone's eyes darted his way. "Why are you laughing?"

"Nothing," Dion said. He looked at his brother. Tyrone got on his last nerve sometimes, but everything his brother had said wasn't exactly a lie. Tyrone only called him out because he cared.

Dion opened his arms. "Come on." He waved his fingers.

Tyrone sucked his teeth but hugged him. Wes slapped them on the back and joined the group hug. "Alright. Now let's go figure out what's going on with this ghost."

The Richardsons weren't thrilled to see Vanessa with Dion and his brothers. She couldn't blame them.

She apologized to them both and promised she was just going to sit back and observe. They accepted her apology, thankfully, and didn't insist she leave. Which is what she expected when she'd seen the look on their faces.

After her apology, Wes went over the equipment they'd use to complete the investigation. Vanessa listened intently as he talked about how an electromagnetic field meter or EMF measured electrostatic energy in the house and how a modified radio app on his phone called a spirit box created white noise ghosts were supposedly able to manipulate.

Vanessa slid closer to Dion as Wes talked to the Richardsons. "Wouldn't the EMF pick up the energy from appliances?" She kept her voice low so as not to interrupt Wes or come across as being biased again.

Dion lowered so he could whisper back in her ear. "It can, and the first thing we do is try to find out if the electrostatic energy people feel is from appliances or if there is an increase in energy from something else."

He was close enough for his breath to tickle her ear, making it impossible to focus on his words. Electric sizzles shot down her neck and across her body. She jerked and turned her head. Only a few inches separated them. Their eyes connected, and Vanessa sucked in a breath. His dark gaze dropped to her lips. Awareness flared and increased the energy humming deep inside her. Dion blinked and leaned back.

Vanessa tried to remember what they'd been talking about. Investigations. Ghosts. Electromagnetic fields. She was surprised the EMF hadn't gone off a second ago.

"Oh…um… That makes sense," she mumbled.

Wesley spoke up. "Let's see what we can find in here, then we'll split up and see what's happening in the bathrooms."

For several minutes Vanessa watched as Wes turned on the EMF and slowly walked around the living room. He introduced himself and the rest of the people in the room and said they just wanted to talk. Vanessa focused on the red light on the EMF, which was supposed to light up with unusual activity.

When nothing happened, the group followed Wes down the hall toward the bedroom. He crossed the threshold, and a loud buzzing sound emanated from the EMF. Vanessa jumped, startled by the abrupt sound. Dion's strong hand pressed into the middle of her back.

"You good?" Concern filled his voice and his eyes.

She felt silly for jumping. "Yeah, I wasn't expecting it to be so loud."

"Hey, we just wanna talk." Wesley spoke this time after everyone crowded into the family's bedroom. "You feel like talking?"

The EMF buzzed and the three brothers grinned like kids in a toy store. Dion pulled out an infrared thermometer. Tyrone slid his phone out of his back pocket. With a few swipes of the screen, the sound of static filled the small space.

"Aight, I'm Tyrone. Are you the spirit that's been hanging out in the Richardsons' house?"

Everyone was quiet as the static echoed in the small space. Vanessa glanced at the ceiling and back at Tyrone and his cell. Was he seriously trying to talk to a ghost through his phone? She crossed her arms and tried to hold back her eye roll when the static changed to something that could be described as a voice for a split second.

Vanessa blinked. Wes, Tyrone and Dion all gasped and bounced on their feet.

"You hear that?" Wes asked.

"I heard, yes." Tyrone glanced at the Richardsons. "Did you hear it?"

Kara pressed a hand to her heart. "I did."

Tyrone asked several more questions. With each change in static, the brothers exchanged excited looks and repeated what they heard just to be sure everyone heard the same thing. While Tyrone asked questions, Dion scanned the room with his infrared thermometer.

"Let's check the bathrooms," Dion said after a few minutes of no further response. "You all check this bathroom and I'll check the guest bath. That's the other place where you felt the presence?"

Kara nodded. "It is."

"Cool. I'll be right back." He looked at Vanessa. "Do you want to check it with me?"

"Sure." She had a bunch of questions and she didn't want to ask them in front of the Richardsons.

They went down the hall to the front bathroom. Once they were out of earshot, she asked, "That wasn't serious, was it?"

"What do you mean?" Dion asked. He had another, smaller EMF in his hand. He waved it slowly back and forth in front of him as they walked down the hall.

"Talking to a ghost through a phone app. It's some kind of trick?"

Dion gave her a perplexed look over his shoulder. "It's not a trick. Are there some phony apps out there? Yes. Mostly the free ones. But Wes always checks out the makers and we only use apps made by people who really want to improve the technology."

"I still don't see how that works," Vanessa said.

"You didn't feel it?"

"Feel what?"

"The change in energy in the bedroom versus out here in the hall? Or notice the cooler temperature at the door of the bathroom?"

She had seen the lower degree reading on his thermometer when he'd scanned that area. "The air-conditioning."

Dion chuckled. "They don't have the air on."

He pushed open the door of the smaller guest bathroom. Vanessa followed him in.

"You okay if I close the door?" he asked.

She shrugged. "Go for it."

He closed the door and without the little bit of light from down the hall they were encased in darkness. Dion's foot stepped on hers. Pain shot through her toe.

"Ouch!"

"My bad. I didn't realize you were so close." His arm brushed her side. "You okay?"

Vanessa shook her foot. "It'll heal before I get married."

"What?"

Vanessa shook her head even though he couldn't see it. "It's something my mom used to say. Whenever we got hurt, she'd always say it would heal before we got married. She was right. At this rate everything I hurt will heal."

She shook out her foot. Dion shifted at the same time and their bodies bumped into each other. His arms shot out to steady her. Vanessa automatically gripped his upper arms. His very strong upper arms. Maybe it was the darkness. Maybe it was a different type of electricity in the air. Maybe it was because she'd wanted to explore the last time she'd touched his arm. The reason didn't matter as she squeezed ever so slightly to see if the muscle gave.

His bicep flexed. His body stilled. The air froze in Vanessa's lungs. Her hands squeezed again. His fingers, which barely grasped her waist, firmed. Emboldened, she ran her hands up his arms to his wide shoulders.

Dion's fingers tugged and she was flush against

his body. Two agonizing seconds passed. Then her chin lifted as his head lowered and their lips touched. The kiss started slowly, hesitantly, with soft, sweet presses of his lips against hers, just enough to make her crave more. Vanessa shifted her head slightly. Dion answered and ran the tip of his tongue against the seam of her mouth. She opened to him. A low moan escaped her as his sweet kiss morphed into an erotic demand.

Her nipples tightened to hard points. Heat pooled between her thighs as Dion's hands dug into her hips, holding her tighter.

The hairs on the back of her neck pricked. The strange feeling of being watched barely registered before the EMF buzzed. Red light filled the small space. Vanessa and Dion jumped apart, their breathing heavy and erratic. Dion turned and scrambled to pick the device off the floor. The bathroom door pushed open. Vanessa yelped and jumped back.

Tyrone held up his hands as if warding off an attack. "Hey... What's going on?"

"Nothing!" Vanessa croaked. "You startled me."

Tyrone's eyes narrowed on them. "I heard the EMF. Did you talk to the spirit, yet?"

Dion cleared his throat. "Nah... We were just about to."

The prickling at the back of her neck wouldn't go away. Vanessa rubbed her neck and shifted her shoulders. "I've got to get some air." She pushed past Dion toward the door. Shaking her head, Vanessa rushed forward. Away from the strange feeling and the urge to kick everyone out of the bathroom so she could take Dion in her arms again.

Chapter Twelve

Dion's cell rang as he closed out the last service request for the day. He cringed and cursed without knowing who called. He didn't feel like talking to anyone. All he wanted was to go home, grab a beer and find something to do around the house to keep him from analyzing what happened between him and Vanessa in that bathroom nearly a week ago.

He'd changed the oil in his truck, replaced the broken boards on his privacy fence and cut every stray piece of grass on his property. The good thing was he handled all the projects he'd put off. The bad thing was no matter how hard he worked when he fell into bed, his mind still drifted to Vanessa's soft lips and the press of her curves against his body.

Dion snatched his phone off his desk and prepared to send whoever was calling directly to voice mail. Until he saw Mrs. Montgomery's name on the phone screen. He couldn't ignore her call.

Dion swiped on the green icon to answer the call. "Hello?"

"Hi, Dion, it's Arletha Montgomery."

He leaned back in his chair. "How are you doing, Mrs. Montgomery?"

"I'm okay. I never did ask how things went up in Columbia with Vanessa."

The memory of a dark room, Vanessa's warm body in his arms, her small fingers squeezing into his biceps filled his mind. Her kiss had been so good. He hadn't had a woman in his arms for way too long, but even if he was living a love-'em-and leave-'em life, her kiss would still be just as good, just as sweet.

Dion shifted in his chair in a vain effort to relieve the pressure rising between his legs. "Uh... Yeah, things went well. Really well. Didn't Vanessa say something?"

Mrs. Montgomery's sigh came through the phone. "She said it was interesting. She admitted you and your brothers seemed to be nice guys."

He perked up. "Does that mean she's okay with us doing the investigation?"

"No, she still thinks everything you all are doing is a bunch of smoke and mirrors. She doesn't want you all investigating my house."

"I understand her concerns, but you know you

can still let us investigate." He didn't want to create tension between her and her granddaughter, but at the end of the day the house belonged to Mrs. Montgomery. The woman knew her own mind and did what she wanted.

"Normally I would, but Vanessa has been through a lot. She's supposed to be here to relax. Instead, she got here and immediately jumped onto this and is worried about me. Honestly, I hoped her opening her mind to the possibility of something new would be good for her. It's why I was excited to see she was willing to go on an investigation with you."

He'd gotten enough from Vanessa to know she'd moved there after losing her job, but he wanted to know more about why she'd shown up. An internet search might tell him something, but he didn't want to search through her private life like some type of stalker.

"What if she's never okay with us investigating?"

"I can deal with Lou until Vanessa is finally out of town. He never hurt me in life and wouldn't hurt me in death. When she's back on her feet and decides to leave, then you boys can come investigate."

Reasonable, but depending on how long she chose to stay they may lose the window to pitch the idea. Tyrone made it seem like his contact wanted to move quickly. What if she changed her mind about the show altogether? As much as he hated admitting Tyrone was right, a small part of Dion was excited about the opportunity. He just wasn't used to dreaming big dreams anymore.

"That brings me to why I called," Mrs. Montgomery interrupted his thoughts.

"What's up?"

"I need a favor. I know you're about to get off work, but if you're not busy, then I could really use your help."

"I don't have any plans. I'm always happy to help you," he said quickly, hoping she'd give him the distraction he needed.

"There's a broken latch on the back screen door to one of my rental houses. I tied it up before the storm the other week, but it really needs to be fixed."

"I'll take care of it, but I thought you always got Henry Jacobs to handle maintenance of your houses."

"I normally do, but Henry had knee replacement surgery a few weeks ago and won't be back up and around for a while. This is such a quick job I figured you could knock it out."

"I've got you." He powered down the computer in his small office he shared with the other crew leaders. "I'll get over there in about an hour."

"Good. While you're there you can keep trying to convince Vanessa."

Dion froze. "Vanessa?" His stomach sank.

Mrs. Montgomery's laughter had a slightly devious undertone. "Oh, didn't I mention it was the house Vanessa is staying in? I guess not. Well, it doesn't

matter. You two are good after the trip, right? Just
send me the bill for any supplies you have to buy."

"Don't worry about paying me," he said automatically. His mind reeled. He'd spent the past few days
trying to forget about Vanessa, that kiss, her curves
pressed against him. Now he was going directly to
her place!

"You're such a good guy, Dion. You know, Vanessa needs a good guy like you in her life. Maybe
you two will hit it off in other ways."

Dion nearly swallowed his tongue. "What?"

"Nothing. Thanks, dear! Call me when you're
done. Bye," she said in a singsong voice before ending the call.

Dion rang the doorbell at Vanessa's place, then
gripped the handle of his toolbox. He shifted from
one foot to the other and rubbed the back of his neck.
He'd go in. Fix the door. Get the hell out of there.

That was it.

No thinking about the kiss. No talking about the
kiss. No overanalyzing the kiss.

As far as he was concerned, the kiss never happened. He didn't want to waste his time. He'd in-
vested in a relationship with a woman who'd left once
before, and he wasn't about to start anything with
Vanessa knowing she was only in town temporarily.
Vanessa was the kind of woman he wouldn't easily
forget. He wasn't starting something destined to fail.

With a deep, reassuring breath, he pressed the

doorbell again. He checked his watch, then looked over to her car parked in the drive. She was there. He wondered if she didn't want him there as much as he didn't want to be there.

The door opened. Dion looked back and forgot how to speak. Vanessa stood on the other side of the screen door. A blanket wrapped around her. Her eyes bloodshot. A wad of balled-up tissue in her hand.

"Hi, D-Dion…" She sniffed and wiped her nose. "Grandma mentioned you were…" She sniffed again. "…coming." Tears filled her eyes and she hastily wiped them away.

Dion opened the screen door and stepped over the threshold. "What's wrong? Are you okay?"

"I'm f-fine," she hiccupped. Swiped a few more tears. Her eyes wouldn't meet his.

"Did you get bad news?" He put the toolbox down and placed a hand on her shoulder. "Do you need anything? Just let me know. I'll get you whatever you need."

She looked up into his eyes. Her lower lip trembled before her face crumpled and tears fell from her eyes. Dion didn't think. He pulled her into his arms and rubbed her back.

"Shh, it'll be okay. Whatever it is. It'll be fine."

He led her from the entryway into the living room. He sat on the couch and pulled Vanessa beside him. Her body shook with her silent tears as he wrapped an arm around her shoulder. She curled into his side. He whispered consoling words, but his body buzzed with the need to find the problem and fix it immediately.

After several long minutes, Vanessa stopped crying. He fought the urge to hold her tighter when she slowly pushed away. He leaned forward and picked up the roll of toilet paper on the coffee table. Dion pulled off a big wad and handed it to her.

"Here you go."

She took the tissue and smiled. "Thank you." She tossed the tattered wad in her hand on the coffee table. "I'm sorry. I didn't mean to do this."

"Really, because I thought you planned to cry and make me comfort you."

Her eyes widened, before she rolled them and grinned. "Yes, my ultimate plan to make you wildly uncomfortable."

He smiled and tapped her knee. "Seriously, you alright?"

"Everything is cool. I just got in my feelings for a moment. It's stupid."

"Nothing's wrong with feeling what you feel. Do you need to talk about it?"

"I'm so sick of talking about it. I'm sick of everyone telling me I'm better off. I'm sick of people giving me sad, pitiful looks and telling me I'll find someone better."

Dion's stomach clenched. This was about a guy. If the asshole made her cry, then he didn't deserve her. He swallowed those words. He remembered what it was like post-breakup. No matter how well meaning, the "you'll find someone better" platitudes weren't comforting.

"That's what people told me after my ex moved out. I still don't like hearing that."

She sat up straighter. "Exactly! I mean, yeah my brain knows I'm better off and I'll find someone better one day, but it still hurts right now."

Her voice didn't falter. She sounded angry. Whoever he was had hurt her, but he hadn't broken her spirit.

"What happened? Between you and the guy?"

She sighed and shook her head. "We broke up the same day I was fired from the station."

Dion cringed. "Damn."

"Exactly."

"Why did you two split?"

She glanced at him out of the corner of her eye, then looked away. "Because his horoscope said he shouldn't commit to a long-term decision and he should consider ending relationships that were going nowhere."

Dion stared, too shocked to believe what she said. "You're lying."

Vanessa snorted. "I wish I were."

"A damn horoscope?" Dion shook his head. What fool dropped a woman like Vanessa over some random words?

She poked his thigh. "You don't believe in astrology?"

Her leg still pressed against his. Now that her

tears were gone he was well aware of her body close to his. Dion shifted away so they wouldn't touch. "Not particularly."

She raised a brow. "But you believe in ghosts?"

"Believing in ghosts and letting a horoscope convince me to break up with a beautiful woman are two different things."

The edges of her lips lifted in a small smile. She glanced away. He shouldn't be flirting, but seeing the light come back to her eyes was worth the small admission.

"I know this doesn't help, but you are better off. Don't waste your tears on him."

She sighed and reached for her cell phone on the coffee table. "I know, but that doesn't make this hurt any less."

She held up her phone. On the screen was a fuzzy picture of a guy in a restaurant with his arms around a woman. The text message beneath it read, "Girl, he's dating that cheerleader."

"Who sent you that?"

"One of my friends from back home." She tossed the phone on the coffee table.

"Sounds like someone stirring up trouble."

Vanessa sighed and glared at her phone. "Maybe, but it confirms my suspicions that the horoscope was an excuse."

"That doesn't make it any less messed up."

"Yep." She tried to smile. "That's why I'm crying. How crappy my life is right now hit me all over again."

"I know how you feel."

She turned and sat cross-legged on the couch facing him. "You do?"

"My ex. We dated for three and a half years. Lived together for the last two. I was ready to settle down, get married, start a family. The first time I proposed she said no because she was going back to school and was touring with her church's gospel choir. She said she was too busy to plan a wedding. I believed her and let it go. The second time I proposed on Valentine's Day. I had the whole setup. Wine, candles, romantic music. I even hired a private chef to come and make her favorite meal. After dinner I pulled out the ring, asked her, and she said she wanted to break things off."

Vanessa gasped and placed her hand over her mouth. "On Valentine's Day?"

Dion nodded. The embarrassment of that moment just as fresh as it had been three years ago. He'd been a fool for not seeing what was obvious for so long.

"She said she didn't want to marry me. That she wanted more out of life than to be the wife of some blue-collar worker. She said I didn't want more and wouldn't be more."

"No, she didn't!" The anger in Vanessa's voice gave him a modicum of comfort.

"Oh, she did. She moved out that weekend. Six

months later, she married one of the guys from her gospel choir. They had their first kid last year."

Her hand slapped his knee. "Forget her."

"I've moved on. If I was honest, I realized we weren't compatible from the start, but I held on. I was trying to be a good man." He rubbed his chin. "Good guys don't always win."

"Yes, they do. You just aren't the good guy for her."

He shrugged. "Maybe one day I'll find the right woman for me."

"And one day I'll find the good guy I deserve."

Their eyes met. His breathing faltered. The memory of her kiss the only thing he could recall. His gaze lowered to her full lips, then back up to the dark depths of her gaze. Something flickered across her face. Something that made him want to pull her into his lap, cover her mouth with his and be the guy she needed right now.

"About the kiss. I'm sorry. I shouldn't have done that," Vanessa said in a rush.

Dion blinked. "You shouldn't have?"

"I know. It was just kind of... I don't know. It was dark, and you were so big."

"Big?" He raised a brow.

She blinked and waved a hand. "I mean... It just kind of happened because of the circumstances. But I'm not going to be here long, and I just got out of a bad breakup, and—"

He raised his hand, not wanting to hear any more

about what a mistake their kiss was. "It's okay, Vanessa. I know it didn't mean anything. We're good."

She nodded. "Good." She licked her lips. "I'd like to go on another investigation with you, if you don't mind."

"Are you starting to believe?"

"No, but I am curious to learn more."

"You could learn more while we investigate your grandmother's house."

"Until I'm comfortable." She held up a finger. "Which I'm not saying I will be. But until then I'd rather just observe first."

"That's fair." He glanced away. "I guess I should fix the door now."

The broken latch was an easy fix. He had it screwed back on in less than fifteen minutes. When he went back inside, Vanessa was in the kitchen. She gave him a shy smile as she held out an insulated paper cup.

"Thanks for the door. And for, you know, letting me cry on your shoulder."

Dion lifted the lid on the cup to the enticing aroma of hot chocolate. "It's no problem at all."

"Do you want to stay for dinner? I could order something."

He did, but he didn't want to get any ideas. She said the kiss was a mistake. She wasn't trying to start something. If he was going to protect his heart, then he needed to keep his distance.

"Nah, I've got food at home. I'll go now."

The light left her eyes. For a second, he thought she'd ask him to stay, but she smiled and nodded. "Cool."

She followed him to the door. Before he left, he turned back to her. "Hey, I don't know your ex, but I do know he's a fool. Any man who would dump a woman like you over a damn horoscope is a fool. You deserve better, Vanessa. I hope one day you find it." He turned and left before she could respond.

Chapter Thirteen

When Sheri texted about having a bonfire at her place, Vanessa had nearly jumped off the couch and driven over immediately. She'd managed to control her answer to a quick "Sure, what do you need me to bring?" reply. She'd spent the three weeks since Dion came over lounging on the beach, looking for jobs and allowing herself to go through the hurt, rage and finally acceptance that washed over her after getting the picture of Daniel and his new girlfriend. Now that she'd gotten that, and him, out of her system, she craved social interaction.

Memories of her last summer in Sunshine Beach kicked in as she drove to the house on the edge of town where Sheri stayed with her mother. Their

bungalow-style home was on an acre lot and surrounded by large oak trees. Dozens of cars were
parked up and down the road. Vanessa found a spot
to squeeze in her rental. She grabbed the pound cake
she'd made after Sheri asked her to bring something sweet and followed the sound of soul music
and laughter.

She rang the doorbell, and Sheri answered the
door. A big smile spread across her face and she
opened her arms. "Yay, you made it." She pulled
Vanessa into a big hug.

"Of course I made it. I've been waiting for someone to do something fun." She hugged her back.

When they pulled back, Sheri took the cake from
Vanessa's hands. "I know. I've been so busy working
all these jobs, but my mom finally found a kidney
donor so it's time to celebrate."

"That's great, Sheri!"

"I know!" Sheri sniffed the cake. "This smells so
good. Did you make it?"

Vanessa nodded. "Yep, I hope it tastes as good as
it smells. I haven't baked in a while. But it's Grandma's recipe."

"Oh, then I know it's good." Sheri nodded toward
the rest of the house. "Come on in and get comfortable. It's mostly family, but I invited friends over,
too. My uncle Tommy already has the low country
boil going, and my auntie Arrie just pulled out the
first batch of fish."

Vanessa's stomach growled in response. "You don't have to tell me twice."

Sheri laughed as she led Vanessa through the house. Vanessa hugged and congratulated her mom, and vaguely remembered some of Sheri's family members from when she'd come over and hung out with her that summer. Before long she was settled at one of the many picnic tables in the backyard with Sheri and several of her female cousins. She listened in as they told stories, laughed and joked.

Sheri's first cousin Cora, the most opinionated of the group, sat up and pointed toward the house. "Lil Bit, you invited Tyrone?"

The ladies gasped and spun around. Sure enough, Tyrone stood there with Dion on his right and Wesley on his left. Vanessa didn't gasp with the rest of the group because of him. Her breath caught when her gaze clashed with Dion's. She'd avoided the early shift at Waffle House to avoid seeing him.

Would he think she was pitiful or pathetic after she'd cried on his shoulder? He'd opened up about his own failed relationship, and she'd appreciated the way he'd listened. Then there were his parting words.

"Any man who would dump a woman like you over a damn horoscope is a fool."

Those words were hard to get out of her head. Damn, if he didn't know how to make a woman feel better. Whoever had left him was a fool.

Sheri let out a heavy sigh. "No, I invited Dion."

"Girl, you know inviting Dion means inviting his

brothers," Cora said. A chorus of "mmm-hmms" followed her statement. "You just want to see Tyrone again."

Sheri rolled her eyes. "Please, you think I want to sign up for that again?"

Cora waved a finger tipped with a bedazzled nail. "I warned you about him when you first moved back."

"What about Dion?" Vanessa asked. When all eyes snapped on her, heat filled her cheeks. "And Wes," she added quickly. "Are they players, too?"

Sheri quickly shook her head. "Wes doesn't really date. Like ever. Dion was with Keisha for a long time. Loved the hell out of that woman."

"And then she ran off with that guy from her gospel choir," Cora said with a twist of her lips. "She's dumb as hell."

Vanessa sipped the grape soda she'd gotten earlier. "Who's he dating now?" She tried to sound nonchalant when she wanted to lean in and soak up every word.

Sheri shrugged. "No one. He's kept to himself. Not for lack of people trying."

Vanessa didn't want to examine why that news made her want to grin.

The three brothers stopped and talked to several people in the backyard, but finally made their way to their table. Dion smiled at everyone there. Cora audibly sighed and giggled. Vanessa couldn't blame her. The man's smile was glorious to behold.

"What's up, ladies?" he said. "Lil Bit, thank you for the invite. I hope you don't mind that I brought my brothers."

"Of course we don't mind having Wes here." Sheri gave Wes a welcoming smile.

The other women chuckled. Tyrone glowered, but smartly kept his mouth shut. Dion held up a bag. "We brought crab legs."

Sheri's eyes lit up. "Then you can bring whoever you want. Come on over here with Uncle Tommy and drop those."

"You got it." Dion grinned at the group of women again. "I'll holla at y'all later."

The women raised their hands and waved. Dion followed Sheri to the place where her uncle and several other people stood around adding shrimp, corn, potatoes and sausage for the low country boil.

Tyrone winked at Cora. "Good seeing you."

The women around the table sucked their teeth and looked away, but Vanessa saw Cora's lips twitching and the way she smoothed her hair.

Wes shook his head and grabbed Tyrone's shoulder. "Come on, man. Let's grab some food." He pulled his brother away.

The women started immediately talking about which brother was the hottest. Vanessa ignored the conversation. Her eyes were stuck on Dion. He'd spoken to the group, but he hadn't given her so much as an extra look or backward glance.

Good. He was listening. She'd said she was just

getting out of a messed-up situation. She didn't need to start a new relationship. Still, they'd spent a weekend together doing an investigation. She'd kissed him. He'd let her cry on his shoulder. She deserved more than a quick hello, right?

Okay, now you're being ridiculous.

Pushing away her disappointment, she tuned back into the conversation. She could ignore him, too. She would ignore him.

She glanced his way again. His eyes were on her. He smiled, lifted his chin and made a quick come-here motion with his head. Vanessa was out of her seat and crossing the lawn without a second thought.

Chapter Fourteen

Dion met her halfway. His feet moved just as quickly as hers. So quickly she wondered if he felt it, too. The pull drawing them together despite both knowing they shouldn't get attached.

"I didn't know you were coming," she said when they met in the middle of the yard.

"Does that mean you wouldn't have shown up if you knew?"

He wore a long-sleeved green shirt that looked good against his dark skin and clung to the muscles of his shoulders and arms. She thought about the last time she'd touched his arm. Explored up to his broad shoulders. Been engulfed by his strong embrace and kissed so good she thought her bones would melt.

She shoved her hands in her pockets to stop herself from reaching out and touching him. "I just mean I wasn't sure if I'd see you."

His lips lifted in a sexy smile that brought out his irresistible dimples. "Do you mind seeing me?"

"Of course not. Why would I?" She lifted her chin and dared him with her gaze to mention her crying on his shoulder.

His broad shoulders lifted and lowered. "No reason. But for real, I thought about you. Are you okay?"

She glanced away. "I'm good."

He shifted until he caught her eye. "Really?"

The concern in his voice softened her defenses. "Really. I don't usually break down like that."

"Sometimes it's good to get it out." There was no judgment in his voice.

"True. I was angry, and wanted to hit something, and yeah a little sad, but overall I'm much better off. I was just telling my mom yesterday that I'm ready to move forward. Get my life back on track."

"Good for you. Does that mean you'll be leaving town soon?"

She tilted her head to the side. "Why? You ready to get rid of me already?"

He chuckled and raised a hand. "Nah, nothing like that. Just hoping I'd get to see you a little more before you left town."

Her heart stuttered. Flirtation filled his eyes. Like a dummy, she answered the call. "I'd like to see more of you, too."

He scratched his chin and nodded. Heat filled her chest. She was aware nothing long term could happen with Dion, but the attraction between them was real. Would a fall fling really be that bad?

"So, what's up with Tyrone and Lil Bit?" she asked before that idea could settle in and make itself comfortable.

Dion groaned. "That's a long story."

"Um… It's not like I'm on a deadline or something. I've got time to hear it."

"I'll just say they hooked up when she came back to town. She thought they were getting serious. Tyrone says he told her he wasn't looking for anything serious."

Her eyes widened. "Was he sleeping around?"

He shook his head. "No. Tyrone gets around, but he's not a cheater. He thought they'd run their course and when he broke it off things didn't go well."

"How not well?"

"Smashed headlight not well."

Vanessa cringed. "Damn."

"Yep."

"And you brought him to her party?"

"That was a year ago. They're not friends, but they're better now. He just didn't expect her feelings to get involved."

Vanessa crossed her arms. "It's why I hate quick flings. Feelings always get caught up. I'm a relationship type of person."

He met her gaze. "And I'm a relationship kind of guy."

She swallowed hard. His eyes promised so much. Promises she knew he'd keep. Promises she'd dreamed of but had yet to find.

Why did it have to be him? She wasn't staying in Sunshine Beach. He didn't seem like the kind of guy willing to tear up his entire life and move to Atlanta. On top of that, he was a paranormal investigator. She'd just gotten out of a bad relationship with one superstitious guy.

"I hope you find that one day," she said.

He rubbed his chin and looked away. "Yeah. Me, too."

She cleared her throat and searched for a safer topic. "I need your help."

"Help with what?"

"I talked to my mom about the ghost—" she made air quotes with her fingers "—at Grandma's house."

"The ghost—" he made air quotes back "—is real and we can make sure it's your grandfather and not someone else."

"Well, before I agree to that, I'd like to learn more. My mom isn't worried about Grandma, and she mentioned all the ghost tours offered around town."

"Yeah?" he said slowly.

"I'd like you to help me pick the right ones. Since you're really into this, I figured you could tell me the best tours and locations to visit."

He shifted his weight and ran a hand over his chin.

"Hold up, you're going to investigate ghosts on your own?"

"No, I'm going to investigate what's happened around those areas. Like you did with the Richardsons. Instead of looking for a ghost, I'm going to look for the reason the legends started in the first place."

He laughed softly. "So you're going to do an exposé to prove they aren't real."

She reached for his arm again, then pulled back. His flexing biceps and that smile were way too tempting. "I just want to learn more about why people believe this."

"And after you investigate, then what?"

She took a deep breath. "Then, I'll let you investigate Grandma's house."

He raised a brow. "Even if you don't believe?"

She nodded. "I saw the worry in the Richardsons' eyes. I don't believe but Grandma does and this will help give her closure. I'd just like to know a little more about all of this."

His eyes narrowed. "And what else?"

Heat flooded her cheeks. The memory of being watched from the other weekend raised the hairs on her neck. She absolutely did not believe, but she couldn't shake the feeling. There had to be another explanation. She couldn't let something go without dissecting it to pieces.

"Nothing. Seriously. I'd like to know more. That's it."

"How long before you make up your mind? Tyrone wants us to pitch the show in a few weeks."

She held out her hand. "I'll let you investigate in time for you to pitch the show."

He still eyed her as if there was more to the story, but finally nodded and took her hand. "Deal."

They pumped twice. Vanessa tried to pull back, but his hand tightened on hers. He tugged gently and she stepped closer. "And at the end of this I'm going to love hearing the words *you were right* come out those lips of yours."

His eyes dropped to her mouth. Heat crackled and popped like the flames of the bonfire. She tried to breathe but the breath was short and shallow. If they weren't in the middle of Sheri's backyard surrounded by her family and friends, she might have closed the distance between them and pressed her lips to his.

Maybe he saw what she wanted because he slid closer. His voice lowered to a rumble. "Your very pretty lips."

Loud laughter rang out from around the bonfire. They dropped hands and spun in that direction. No one looked their way. All eyes were focused on someone telling a story.

Vanessa pressed a hand to her belly and stepped away from Dion. "Well… I doubt you'll hear that. I'm just satisfying my curiosity. Not searching for evidence of real ghosts."

"Sure, Vanessa." His voice held some humor.

"I'll start by visiting that house you told me about. The one you and your brothers went to."

His eyes narrowed. "I thought you said we were stupid for spending the night at that place."

She pointed at him. "You were stupid." She pointed to her chest. "I'm not. I'm going in broad daylight."

He shook his head. "Don't go out there by yourself."

"Why not?"

"Because that house is old and hazardous. Plus, the dirt roads leading there are bad and become a bog if it starts raining."

"Then I'll go on a sunny day."

All humor left his face. "I'm serious, Vanessa. Don't go out there by yourself. Promise me."

She crossed her arms. He'd gotten that I'm-the-boss voice she'd heard him use with his brothers. The voice that thrilled and irritated her. She'd investigated situations more serious and scarier than an old house. While she appreciated Dion's concern, she could take care of herself.

She pointed toward the bonfire. "Let's go hear what's so funny."

Dion's hand wrapped around hers. "Promise." His voice softened. Concern entered his eyes. As if he didn't know what he'd do if something happened to her. The look tugged on something in her heart. She didn't want to follow the string to see where it led.

"It's all good, Dion." She shook off his hand and turned away.

* * *

Dion couldn't forget the look in Vanessa's eyes when he'd asked her to promise not to visit the old house. Or her flippant "It's all good" before dragging him over to the bonfire. She didn't seem the type to put herself in unnecessary danger. If she didn't believe him, she surely would have asked someone else about the bad roads leading out there. Surely if she still chose to go she wouldn't go alone.

He hadn't been able to get time alone with her at the bonfire and bring it up again. He hadn't been able to sleep with thinking about Vanessa going out alone. That's why he was up early and at Waffle House for coffee and eggs on a Saturday. He usually slept in on the weekend, but something urged him to get out of the house. Plus, Vanessa visited the restaurant on weekend mornings too. Maybe he'd get a chance to try to talk her out of going by herself.

"Hey, Dion," Sheri said when he walked through the door.

At eight in the morning on a Saturday, the restaurant was busier than his usual time at four on a weekday. Instead of snagging his usual booth, he settled for one of the barstools near the register.

"I didn't expect to see you here this morning. Not after the party you threw last night."

She chuckled and came over with a pot of coffee in one hand and placed a mug in front of him. "I didn't plan to come in. I planned to sleep in late, but Rose's daughter is sick and when Earl called and asked if I'd take the shift I agreed." She poured coffee into the mug.

"You deserve a raise," Dion said.

She pointed at him. "I do. Make sure you tell Earl that the next time he comes through."

"I will."

Sheri placed a hand on her hip. "Why did you all dip out so early yesterday?"

Dion poured sugar into the coffee and shrugged. "You know I go to bed early."

She chuckled. "You better stop before you get old too soon."

The words hit a sore spot. This wasn't the first time he'd heard his early bedtime was acting too old for his age.

"Is that why I don't have a woman?" he asked with a half smile.

"Dion, please. You know half the women in this town are ready for you to get back on the dating scene. Don't even act like you're one of those nice guys that finish last."

He grunted and sipped his drink. At his last check, he *was* a nice guy who finished last. Sure, there were women who'd expressed interest, and some had outright asked him if he wanted to go out, but eventually they'd lose interest. Move on to someone better and more exciting.

"Unfortunately, the women in town will have to wait a little longer," Sheri said with a raised brow.

"Because I saw you yesterday and I know there's something simmering between you and Vanessa."

She drifted away before he could respond to that. There was nothing going on with him and Vanessa. Well, there was that kiss, but she'd said it was a mistake. That and she obviously wasn't over her ex.

When Sheri came back after helping her other customers, she asked if he was ready to order.

"For the record, there's nothing going on with me and Vanessa."

Sheri didn't look convinced. "You sure?"

"Very sure. Besides, she's leaving town soon."

"That doesn't mean anything. And the way she was going on this morning about you."

He sat up straighter. "She was here this morning?"

"Yeah, came in about thirty minutes before you got here. She was asking for directions to the Bookersville house. She said you told her not to go but insisted she could take care of herself. I could tell you got under her skin telling her what to do."

"What?" His voice rang out and caused several people to stop talking and look his way.

Sheri blinked. "She's going to the Bookersville place."

"Today?" Dion glanced out at the sky. "It's supposed to rain today."

"Later today. She said she's just driving by and will be out of there before the rain started."

Dion looked out the window again. Dark clouds gathered on the horizon. "This afternoon my ass.

That rain is coming early." He jumped up. "She's so damn stubborn."

"And you're going after her?"

"You know how those roads get when it rains."

Sheri grinned knowingly. "You're going to rescue her?"

"It's not a rescue. I'm just making sure she gets out of there okay."

"Sounds like a rescue to me."

He glared and reached for his wallet. Sheri raised a hand. "The coffee is on me today."

"Thanks," he said and turned to run out. Sheri's *"I knew something was going on"* echoed in his ears.

Chapter Fifteen

Vanessa parked in the overgrown drive that ended in front of the dilapidated house. Green mold and overgrown vines covered the outside of the two-story structure. The stairs leading up to the house didn't look as if they could support a squirrel much less a person. All the windows were broken. In the daylight the place looked like any other abandoned home. The gathering clouds in the distance gave the place a foreboding air.

Dion's warning rang in her ear. Not because of the potential for ghosts, but because walking into any abandoned home that had obviously been ignored for decades wasn't a good idea. She should turn around right now and head back home before the rain hovering on the horizon came in.

Except, something about the place made her turn off the engine and get out. She wanted to know more about what had drawn Dion and his brothers here in the first place. She, personally, didn't want to ever find proof ghosts existed. Not just because it would more than likely scare the crap out of her, but because she'd have to rethink everything she ever thought was true. If ghosts were real, then what else she'd considered fantasy was real.

No, she would prove this was all superstition. She'd only go in for a few minutes. The storm wasn't there yet, so there was plenty of sunlight, for now. Even if she did believe in ghosts, television and movies proved she should be safe in daylight. Ghosts only attacked at night. Right?

Pushing that thought aside, Vanessa got out of the car, grabbed her notebook and cell phone and headed toward the house. The front door was already cracked open. Probably because the house was abandoned, and anyone could come in whenever they pleased.

Inside was as she expected. Dust coated the floors and cobwebs thick as wool blankets filled every corner. No furniture adorned the rooms that branched off the entryway. Evidence of the people who visited before was everywhere. Footsteps in the dust, an old kerosene lantern, the dusty remnants of a blanket and soda cans, beer bottles and potato chip bags littered the floor.

Vanessa walked through the downstairs. She stood

still and listened in each room. She didn't know what she expected to hear, but all she heard was the wind outside. No quiet whispers of unsettled spirits. No cool spots. No feeling as if eyes watched her. Maybe the rats watched her. Their droppings in the corners proved they occupied the space.

The sound of thunder in the distance made her check her watch. She glanced out the broken windows at the darkening sky, then at the stairs leading to the second floor. She didn't expect to find anything different upstairs, but she didn't want to leave without checking out the entire house. Just to prove, unequivocally and without a doubt, that there were no such things as ghosts in this home. She had time to do a quick sweep of the upstairs and leave before the storm came.

A louder, closer clap of thunder made the house shake. Her steps quickened. The stairs creaked under her weight. It was an old house. It was going to creak. Still, her unease grew with each wobbly step, and a vision of the holes in the stairs leading to the house filled her mind.

"Be positive, Vanessa," she said to herself. "Plenty of people have been here. You know they went upstairs."

She took a confident step forward. The wood creaked, then gave way beneath her foot. She stumbled onto the stairs. Her hands flew out to brace her fall. Pain shot through her palms, knees and hip as she fell forward. Her cell phone tumbled down the stairs. Dust flew everywhere, clogging her nose and mouth. She sneezed and waved her hands in a feeble attempt to make the dust settle.

Once the sneezing stopped and her heart settled, she took stock of her predicament. Her left leg had gone through the stair up to her thigh. Her right ankle throbbed. She was sore, winded and, as she tugged on her leg with no budging, apparently stuck.

"Dammit!" she groaned and hit the stairs with her fist. She tried to pull her leg out of the hole. Pain shot through the back of her thigh.

"Ouch!" She twisted to look behind her. A jagged piece of the wood she'd broken through pressed into the back of her thigh.

Vanessa let out a pitiful groan. "You had to check out the upstairs, didn't you, Vanessa," she muttered. Her phone was out of reach, she was stuck in a hole, and the only person who knew she was here was Sheri, who wouldn't have a reason to tell anyone. She could almost hear Dion's *I-told-you-so*.

Vanessa tugged on her leg again. The wood dug in deeper. She clenched her teeth. If she jerked hard enough she might get loose, but she'd also end up with a huge gash on the back of her leg from a suspect piece of wood.

"Gash or being stuck here all day. You decide," she said with determination she didn't feel.

She closed her eyes and gave a mental *you can do it* pep talk and countdown. Something brushed across her ankle in the hole. Vanessa's eyes popped open. "What the hell was that?"

Her only answer was another brush across her ankle. A vision of the rat droppings on the first floor, quickly followed by dark beady eyes checking out her exposed ankle like an all-you-can-eat buffet, flashed through her head. The third brush was firmer and cold. Vanessa screamed and jerked on her leg. Pain be damned, she was not about to lose a foot to a hungry rat.

The door downstairs crashed open. "Vanessa!"

The sound of Dion's voice brought tears of relief to her eyes. "Up here. On the stairs. I'm stuck."

Dion's footsteps pounded across the floor in her direction. When he reached the bottom of the stairs, she twisted to look over her shoulder at him. "Wait, the stairs are weak. You'll fall through."

Dion waved her words away. "I know which ones to avoid." He tentatively but quickly climbed to her, his feet avoiding certain stairs and landing in what appeared to be firmer areas on the ones he did step on. "Are you okay? I heard you screaming."

"I screamed because something is touching my foot. Get me out. Please!" She didn't care if she begged. She did not want to be trapped here any longer than necessary.

"I've got you." Dion's voice was calm, soothing. He sat next to her and took in the situation before easily ripping away the piece of wood pushing into the back of her leg. He tossed it over the railing. "Can you lift up?"

Vanessa stared at him dumbfounded for a second. He'd torn a piece of wood with all the effort it took her to rip a Band-Aid. A ray of light broke through the gathering clouds outside and filtered in the broken window, surrounding Dion's head in a golden halo. Her heart flipped over in her chest.

"Vanessa." Dion snapped his fingers in front of her face. "You okay? Can you move?"

She blinked and heat filled her cheeks. She tugged on her leg and this time it moved. She struggled to get herself free. Dion put his hands on her hips and eased her out of the hole and onto his lap. Vanessa gasped and gripped his shoulders. His very firm shoulders. The heat in her cheeks spread to her neck and chest.

"Oh…um…"

"Do you need me to carry you down or can you walk?" Concern filled his voice and his chocolate brown eyes.

She wanted him to carry her down the stairs. She was quite sure he'd be able to do that without breaking a sweat. The heat lowered to her midsection and settled at the juncture of her thighs. Her breasts felt heavy and she was keenly aware that the side of one of them brushed against his chest.

Dion moved to get up with her in his arms. Vanessa shook her head. "I can walk. I can walk." Her voice trembled.

She scrambled to get up out of his lap. Dion stood and placed his hand on her waist before she could take off down the stairs. His grip was strong and sure. The warmth of his palm seared her hip through her jeans. She bit her lip to stop the embarrassed giggle tickling her throat.

"Hold up," he said. "You don't need to get stuck again. Follow me down."

She nodded because she didn't trust her voice. She glanced down into the hole where she'd been stuck, expecting to see the reflection of rat eyes. Nothing was there. Thunder clapped closer and louder this time, followed by the sound of heavy rain. Vanessa jerked and shivered.

Dion held out his hand, and she took it without hesitation. She followed him down the stairs. She winced as the pain in her bruised and battered legs increased. When they made it down the stairs, her palm was sweaty in Dion's grasp and her teeth clenched.

He glanced at her on the way to the door. The concern was still there but something else simmered behind the concern. His dark eyes lowered to her legs and back to her face.

"I'm okay," she said.

"It's raining and outside is nothing but mud. It'll be even harder for you to walk." With little effort, he swept her into his arms and took long determined steps out of the house.

Raining was an understatement for the torrential

downpour falling from the sky. The wind bent the trees. Fat raindrops belted them as they stood on the dilapidated porch. Dion rushed down the stairs and jogged the short distance to his truck parked next to her small sedan. His quick sprint didn't stop them from getting drenched by the time he opened the passenger side door and dropped her onto the seat. He ran around the truck and got in on the driver's side.

"What about my car?" she asked.

"The roads out of here are going to be hell to drive in this rain. That little thing won't make it," he replied in a hard voice.

"How did you know I was here?"

"Lil Bit told me." He shifted in the seat and glared at her. "Why did you come up here by yourself? I told you not to come by yourself. Do you know what could have happened to you? What if I hadn't gone to the Waffle House? You would have been stuck up here for God knows how long. Dammit, Vanessa, you could have hurt yourself. I get it. You're a strong, independent woman who doesn't need someone telling her what to do. I respect that. I just need you to also respect your safety enough to listen to reason. I don't know what I would have done…" He closed his eyes. His nostrils flared with his deep heavy breaths. When he opened his eyes, they were angry and pleading. "Don't do this crap again. Do you understand me? Don't put yourself in danger just to prove something. You hear me?"

Vanessa's breathing shortened with each word.

She was infuriated he thought he could scold her like a child, but beneath that fury something else simmered. A fire that started when he'd jerked away the piece of wood trapping her and had grown as he'd carried her out of the house and to the safety of his vehicle. Her eyes dropped to his full lips, broad shoulders and the muscles of his arms straining as he tried to hold back his anger and frustration at having to come find her. Slick heat pooled between her legs and she pressed her thighs together.

"Vanessa," he snapped. "Do you hear me? Are you okay?"

"I'm more than okay," she said, then lunged forward and pressed her lips to his.

Chapter Sixteen

Dion's brain scrambled to catch up with what was happening. The fear that gripped his heart after hearing her scream coalesced with the thought of her being stuck there for who knew how long if he hadn't arrived and morphed into a frustrated anger he didn't know what to do with. He hadn't meant to lash out at her. He'd expected her to snap back. Tell him to mind his business. Remind him that she could take care of herself.

He had not expected her to press those luscious lips against his. For her fingers to cup the sides of his face and pull him closer. For her to let out the softest, most seductive whimper he'd ever heard as she brushed his lower lip with the tip of her tongue.

Reason and logic said kissing Vanessa right now after she'd just been through a scary situation wasn't right. That he should focus on getting them back to the main road before the storm got too bad. Reason and logic could kiss his ass.

Dion pressed his hand to the back of her head and parted his lips. Vanessa's tongue slid into his mouth. She tasted so sweet. The blood rushed from his head, creating an addictive buzz that only made him crave more. His skin tingled and his toes curled. He was instantly captivated by the taste of Vanessa's lips.

She kissed him with no shyness or hesitancy. Her hands dropped to his shoulders and her nails dug as she grabbed his shirt. The pain combined with the pleasure of her kiss. Dion swelled uncomfortably against the zipper of his jeans. He'd thought about having her lips on his in the weeks since they last kissed. Thoughts and memories couldn't compare to the real thing.

Vanessa let out another soft moan. The sexy sound made him want to rip off her clothes and bury himself deep enough to find out how loud she would get. The image of being inside her fed his desire. His fingers pulled on her hair and tugged her head back. His lips left hers and dropped to her neck, where he kissed and sucked on the soft skin there. Her perfume, sweet like peaches, filled his senses and drove his craving.

She gasped and pulled on his shirt. Kissing her

wasn't enough. He had to touch her, feel every single inch of her body. Discover every delicious part of her. His other hand gripped her waist. Her shirt shifted enough for his fingers to brush the bare skin of her side. He shoved his hand up her shirt and splayed his fingers across her lower back, pulling her even closer into his embrace.

One of Vanessa's hands dropped from his shoulder to his thigh. She squeezed the hard muscle before her hand slid closer to his crotch. Good God, yes! His entire body tightened in anticipation. He brought his mouth back to hers and kissed her with even more urgency than before. Her sweet fingers shifted closer to where he wanted them before they dug into his thigh again.

His hand shifted up her back to the clasp of her bra. With a few deft moves, he had the clasps unhooked. Vanessa sucked in a breath and let out the sweetest moan that turned his body into a tuning fork. He quickly shifted his hand to the front and pulled the underwire away from her chest. The heavy weight of her full breasts spilled out. He trembled with the first gentle squeeze. Her nipples were so damn hard. She squirmed and let out more of those hypnotizing moans and whimpers each time his thumb brushed them.

He had to see them. Had to taste them. Had to have more of her.

Thunder boomed, lightning flashed and his truck shook. Dion and Vanessa jerked back. The sound of their ragged breathing nearly drowned out the pounding rain outside.

Vanessa's eyes didn't leave his. Her lips were wet and swollen. Her breast still in his hand. Every part of his body, most especially the rock-hard erection between his legs, pushed him to kiss her again. Her dark eyes melted and she leaned closer to him.

Thunder rumbled again. Dion closed his eyes and shook his head. This was not the place. He'd had sex in a truck before and as fun as it could be, that was not the way he wanted Vanessa. He wanted her spread out, naked, on a bed where he could explore every inch of her body.

"We need to get out of here." His voice was rough and firm with the effort it took for him to stop what they started.

Vanessa pulled back quickly, taking the soft heat of her breast from his hand along with her sweet scent. He opened his eyes to find her pushing the hair behind her ears before struggling to get her bra arranged. He wanted to tell her to leave it off, ride with them free, and slide across the seat into the crook of his arm so he could steer the car with one hand and massage one with the other.

His dick flexed. Dion groaned and tried to rearrange his erection into a more comfortable position. Not easy when there was no chance of it going down for the length of this car ride.

"Vanessa…um…"

She pulled on her seat belt and avoided eye contact. "Let's go before the storm gets worse."

Did she regret what happened? The thought unleashed a host of insecurities he didn't want to face. After she kissed him like that, there was no way he could pretend as if he didn't want to kiss her again. He opened his mouth to ask when another clap of thunder shook the truck and made her jump. Now was not the time. He'd figure out a way to find out what was going on in her head during the ride back. He nodded, put the truck in gear and started the tedious trek back to the main road.

They rode in silence for nearly twenty minutes. The storm pelted rain, so Vanessa chose silence rather than to distract Dion as he focused on the roads. The quiet also gave her time to calm down her hormones. Something extremely hard to do when the effects of Dion's touch and kisses lingered long after he'd pulled away. The spot on her neck where he'd sucked throbbed, her breasts ached, her panties were wet.

She shifted in the seat and darted another glance in his direction. His hands clenched the steering wheel. He focused on the road ahead of him. They were now entering town and leaving the bumpy dirt roads behind. Thankfully, the storm was letting up.

She wanted to know his thoughts. He had to be thinking about that kiss just as much as she was. There was no way he could kiss her like that and not think about it. The man had unhooked her bra in record time and with ease.

Her eyes narrowed and she glanced at him again. Why did he know how to unhook a bra so easily? Dion came across as the responsible, good guy of the three brothers. Not that good guys didn't unhook bras, but he'd done it with efficiency. Was he all nice and noble on the surface but an expert with his hands in the bedroom?

Warmth spread across her cheeks, chest and midsection. That was not the right place to let her thoughts go. The idea of Dion being a low-key sex god was too tempting. She looked at his hands on the steering wheel and imagined them going across her skin, cupping her breasts, sliding between her legs.

"What's wrong?" Dion's tight words snapped her out of the fantasy.

Vanessa blinked and cleared her throat. She looked out the front windshield and shook her head. "Nothing."

He was quiet for several seconds before he shifted. His fingers tightened on the steering wheel. "So, what happened?"

"What do you mean what happened?" she asked in a rush. Did he want some rational explanation for why she'd kissed him? Because, she didn't have one.

"At the house? Before you fell through the stairs." A touch of humor entered his voice with the last part.

Now that the immediate shock was over, it was slightly humorous. Her shoulders relaxed. "Nothing happened. I looked around downstairs. Saw the trash people left behind but that was the scariest thing there. I wanted to check out the upstairs quickly before the storm came through and… Well, my foot went through the stairs."

He shook his head. "People don't go upstairs," he said as if she should know that.

"Why not?"

"For one, the stairs aren't safe." He gave her a told-you-so side-eye. "You have to be very careful going up and know where to put your foot."

She rolled her eyes. He could have told her that yesterday. "What else?"

"What else what?"

"You said for one. Is there another reason?"

He lifted a shoulder. "Most of the bad encounters happen upstairs. It's one of the reasons people don't go up. The spirits seem okay if you're downstairs. They make their presence known and observe. But upstairs, they tend to be more protective of that space and don't tolerate the intrusion."

Despite herself, Vanessa shivered. Maybe it was a good thing she'd fallen through. She pushed that thought aside. Feeling relieved only gave credence to the idea that spirits were real. She did not believe they were. At all.

"Why were you screaming? Did they bother you?"

She would have reminded him she didn't believe in anything supernatural, except the worry in his voice stopped her. She didn't feel like teasing him about his part-time passion. Dion was like her in many ways. He wanted to solve problems and help people. The same reason she'd become a reporter.

"Something was on my foot. It was cold and wet and all I could picture were the owners of those rat droppings scurrying beneath the stairs and eyeing my ankle as their next meal."

"It probably wasn't a rat," he said matter-of-factly.

The sensation against her ankle came back in cold clarity and Vanessa crossed her arms tightly. "Don't. It's bad enough to think of it as a rat. I don't need anything else in my brain right now."

He glanced over at her. The corner of his lips lifted in a crooked smile that made her melt like chocolate. "Fine. We'll go with a rat." The smile faded to a serious look. "Nothing else happened. You're okay?"

She nodded. "I'm good. I was afraid when I fell. I dropped my phone and…oh crap!"

His eyes widened and darted her way. "What?"

"I left my phone. It fell down the stairs and I forgot about it in the rush to get out."

He relaxed against the seat. "Don't worry. I'll get it and your car."

"You don't have to do that. I can get—"

"Vanessa, I get it. You don't want to ask for help, but the roads are terrible out there, so instead of giving me all the reasons why you can do this on your own, which are valid, just relax and let me help you out. It's not a problem. Seriously."

He'd gotten that authoritative, confident tone again. The tone that should have made her spine stiffen. Not make her want to kiss him again.

She held up her hands in surrender. "Okay, you can help me get my car and phone."

"Thank you."

He turned onto Spring Street. Vanessa wasn't ready for their time to end. She wanted to crawl in his lap and finish what they'd started. He hadn't mentioned the kiss and now seemed blasé about the entire thing. Did this man not know the effect he had on women? Or, worse, what if he knew the effect and just didn't want to have that effect on her?

Dion pulled into the driveway. The rain still came down steadily. Her clothes were damp from the mad dash through the rain earlier. She let out a disappointed sigh at the idea of getting wet again.

"I've got an umbrella in the back." He leaned over to the backseat.

The movement brought him closer to Vanessa. His T-shirt strained over the muscles of his chest as he reached. The tips of his flat nipples were visible through the damp material. Vanessa licked her lips. It would be so easy to lean forward and press her lips against…

"Here you go." Dion slid forward with the umbrella in his hand.

Vanessa stared at the blue-and-white-striped umbrella, then back to his face. His expression was neutral. Was he really going to send her inside with just the umbrella and a goodbye? Her desire waned and she felt foolish.

She grabbed the umbrella and held it to her chest. "Um…thanks. I'll give it back when you get the car."

"How's your leg?"

"It's okay. I can make it inside." She fumbled with the door.

"You should get someone to look at it. Your pants were ripped. I don't know if it was small scratch or a bigger cut."

She glanced over his shoulder. "You want to look at it for me?" The words tumbled out before she could think them over.

Dion's body stilled. The neutral expression on his face slipped. Hunger, raw and potent, flashed in his dark eyes. "You don't want me to do that." Decadent promise filled his voice.

The air in the truck crackled with energy. Vanessa wasn't sure how they'd switched from casual conversation into high intensity, but she wasn't about to turn back. "Why not?" she asked with a raised brow.

"Because if I come inside and check your leg, I'm not stopping there. I'm going to check every single inch of your body."

Vanessa's breathing stuttered. Even though she was only in town temporarily and she wasn't ready to get into another relationship, Dion examining every single inch of her body would be worth every damn second. "Then let's go do that."

Chapter Seventeen

Dion held the umbrella for Vanessa as they walked to the front door. One hand rested on the small of her back as she tried not to limp with her sore ankle. The warmth from his body warded off the chill from the wind and rain. She wanted to curl into his arms and ask him to carry her to the door, but she had some self-control. She fumbled to pull the keys from her pocket. She was thankful she'd put them in her pocket and hadn't lost them when she'd fallen.

Dion's hand dropped from her back. She felt his gaze on her as she unlocked the door. Tension grew with each passing second. He'd promised to check every single inch of her body, yet his behavior was patient and steady just like always. She, on the other hand, was ready to strip naked the second they got through the door.

Dion left the umbrella on the porch and followed her inside. Vanessa pushed back her hair, frizzy thanks to the rain, and faced him in the entryway. Standing there with her torn pants, wild hair and wrinkled clothes she imagined she looked like a wet cat who'd just gotten into a fight. She'd never been unsure or shy when it came to sex but she wasn't some fantastic seductress, either. She liked for a guy to take the lead or to at least know he was just as anxious to get to the bedroom as she was.

"There's a first aid kit in the bathroom." She pointed over her shoulder. "I can go get it." She looked up into his eyes and her breathing stopped.

The passion in Dion's eyes set her body on fire. "I don't need a first aid kit." He took two steps forward, placed one hand behind her head and kissed her with all the hunger of a man obsessed.

Vanessa lifted onto her toes and pressed her hands against his chest. Not to push him away, but to feel the hard muscles beneath his shirt. His heart pounded beneath her palms. Vanessa's own heart soared. He may be calm and controlled on the outside, but Dion was just as excited. She lost herself in the kiss, his embrace, the need pulsing through her veins.

She pulled up his shirt. Wanting it off so she could see and touch him without any barrier. He pulled back enough to pull the T-shirt off and toss it aside. Vanessa's eyes widened and she grinned at the wide expanse of dark skin and thick muscle covered with curly hair.

"I'm supposed to be examining you," Dion said with a half grin.

"Sorry, but these have been teasing me since the car," she said.

Dion frowned. "What?"

Vanessa leaned forward and ran her tongue across one of his flat nipples. Dion's body shivered and he let out a shaky breath through clenched teeth. His fingers dug into the back of her hair. She grinned and flicked her tongue again.

"Damn, Vanessa." Dion's voice was rough and shaky. He lightly pulled on her hair to get her to back off.

Vanessa gasped and let him pull her back. He jerked on her shirt and she lifted her arms. Slowly, he eased the shirt off her body, the damp material brushing across her sensitive skin. Her top joined his on the floor before his mouth covered hers in a hot kiss. Dion's fingers worked their magic and unhooked her bra. The bra's support gave way and her breasts fell free. His big hands caressed them perfectly.

"These have teased me since the moment I first met you," he said in a thick voice. He backed her up against the wall. His head lowered. His lips trailed across her neck, shoulders and chest before the warmth of his mouth engulfed one nipple. He palmed the other with his hand, massaging and teasing the sensitive tip while he sucked on the other with just enough pressure to drive her wild.

Pleasure rushed from where his lips and tongue tantalized her to every part of her body. Vanessa moaned and pushed forward. He dropped his hand and Vanessa groaned.

"Don't stop."

"Who said I'm stopping?" he answered and took her other breast in his mouth. With his free hand, he unbuttoned her pants and drew down the zipper. He pushed them over her hips, then stepped back so she could step on the hem and lift her leg to pull them off.

His eager fingers jerked on her panties. The sound of seams splitting made her gasp. "You ripped my panties."

"I'll buy you more," he said, not sounding the least bit remorseful.

His hand moved across her thighs before settling into the slick folds of her sex. Vanessa forgot about her panties. She had plenty more. His forefinger circled then grazed her swollen clit before pushing deep inside her. Vanessa moaned and clutched his broad shoulders. His mouth never left her breast as he repeated the motion. Over and over, steadily until her entire body shook. She was dangerously close, and she did not want to come from his finger. Not when there was a rock hard penis attached to Dion's body.

"Dion..." His finger pushed inside her, and his thumb rubbed her clit. "Oh God, Dion don't you dare make me come. Not yet."

He lifted from her breast and smiled a wicked smile. "Why not?" He continued to push in and out of her with that long, wicked finger.

"I didn't ask you in here to get me off with your finger. You know what I want."

His finger slid out slowly where he traced her entrance. "What do you want?" He slid back in slowly.

Vanessa's lids lowered. Her head fell back, and her body trembled. She bit her lip and lightly punched his shoulder. "Stop playing with me."

He raised a brow as if just realizing what she wanted. "Oh, you want something bigger and thicker than this." He pushed two fingers inside her.

Vanessa's eyes rolled to the back of her head. She hit his shoulder harder. "Dion." She half moaned and half whined.

He leaned forward and whispered in her ear, "Please tell me you have condoms."

She nodded frantically. "Yes. Master bath. Medicine cabinet."

He lifted her in his arms so fast her head spun. A few seconds later, they were in the bathroom. Dion sat her on the cold counter and yanked open the medicine cabinet. Items flew as he rummaged through the contents. He found the box, ripped off the top and tore off a foil packet.

Vanessa watched with her lips between her teeth as he shoved down his pants and underwear. His thick erection bounced free and she had to stop herself from squealing in delight. She could not wait to have that all up inside her. Dion didn't even kick off his pants. He kept them around his ankles as he rolled the condom on. When he looked back up at her, she gasped. The raw hunger in his eyes sent a rush of wetness to her core. She clenched the walls of her sex but only felt empty.

Dion pushed her legs open, grasped her waist and pulled her forward while his other hand guided his erection right into her slick sex. They both moaned and sat for a second as the bliss of him stretching and filling her washed over them. But only a second.

He grabbed her waist with both hands, pulled back almost to the tip and plunged back inside her to the hilt. The pleasure was exquisite. Vanessa cried out and braced her hands on the counter. Otherwise, his deep strokes would push her back into the wall. He made love to her hard and fast. The strokes deep and long and just what she needed. Vanessa's head fell back and her eyes closed. His warm lips closed over her nipple. One hand left her waist and pushed up her breast so he could take the tip in deeper.

"Oh God!" Vanessa moaned.

She watched him through her lashes. Everything about him took her breath away. He was so big, bold and beautiful yet he was still disciplined, tender and strong. He made love to her with so much passion, but still touched her as if she were precious. Her legs wrapped around his waist and she clenched her sex around him.

"Ah, damn, Vanessa." He rose up and grabbed her

hips again. He bit his lower lip and looked at her with barely constrained control in his dark eyes. His hips rotated with his next push and her legs quivered.

"Touch yourself," he said in a low voice.

Her face heated. The primal need in his sexy voice had her lifting one hand from the counter. Her fingers circled her sensitive clit. Dion's steady thrusts continued. Vanessa's toes curled and pressure built. His eyes dropped to where they were connected and narrowed. He licked his lips and Vanessa exploded.

Chapter Eighteen

Dion's cell vibrated in his pocket as he loaded equipment onto the back of his work truck. He hastily pulled out the phone hoping to see Vanessa's number, then immediately realized her phone was still out at the Bookersville place.

"Calm down, man," he mumbled to himself and answered Wesley's call.

"Hey, we're out front," Wesley said.

"I'll be right there." He turned to his crew chief, Bobby. "I've got to give something to my brother. I'll be right back."

Bobby gave him a thumbs-up. "No problem. We'll finish loading the truck."

Dion nodded and walked toward the main building. He'd hoped to spend the rest of Saturday night and the majority of Sunday in bed with Vanessa. They'd showered, and he'd treated the scratch on her leg when his cell phone rang.

The storm had knocked over trees and flooded a few roads. Dion and his crew were called in. He'd left a naked and very tempting Vanessa, wrapped in a robe, on the bed.

He'd fallen immediately asleep when he'd gotten home late that night. Only to get up the next morning and complete the work. Despite his busy schedule, he hadn't forgotten his promise to her. He'd asked Wes and Tyrone to pick up Vanessa's car and phone. It had taken a little finagling, but they'd agreed.

He walked through the main administrative building where the director and other administrative and technical employees in the department were located. Their building was brighter, cleaner and a lot quieter than the garage. Especially on a Sunday when only a few people were working the storm response.

He went through the front glass doors and spotted Wesley's SUV pulled up to the curb in front of the building. Dion walked over to the passenger side, where Tyrone sat.

Tyrone let down the window. "Eh, man, since when did we become Vanessa's errand boys?"

Dion pulled Vanessa's car key from his pocket and held it out. "Since I offered to help her get the car."

Wesley turned in his seat with one arm resting

on the steering wheel. He gave Dion a curious look. "Why is her car up there anyway?"

Dion leaned a hand on the rearview mirror. "She went to check out the place for ghosts."

Tyrone shook his head. "Say what?"

"Why?" Wesley asked.

"She's trying to figure out why we do what we do. She went up there yesterday morning, but the storm came in and she was stuck."

Tyrone's brows drew together. "So, she called you to come get her?"

"No, I went up there after I found out she'd gone. You know people not familiar with the house shouldn't be roaming around."

Wesley's eyes lit up. "Oh, you decided to go play superhero."

"Hell yeah he did," Tyrone agreed with a grin.

His brothers laughed and Dion reached in and pushed Tyrone's head. "I went to make sure nothing happened. Good thing I did. She tried to go upstairs."

His brothers immediately sobered. They'd visited that house more than enough to know about the hazards around the place.

Tyrone sat forward. "What happened?"

"Nothing, she fell through the stairs. Hurt her leg and twisted her ankle. Then the storm came in, so I got her out of there quick. We didn't have a way to get her car and she forgot she'd dropped the phone until we were back at her place."

Wesley's shoulders relaxed. "I'm glad she's okay."

Tyrone nodded. "Yeah, she's good, right?"

"She's fine." More than fine. He thought about not just the sex on the counter but the way she'd dropped to her knees in the shower and taken him in her mouth. He'd never wanted to give a woman everything he owned before that moment. He didn't know how he'd avoided collapsing after she pulled his very soul from his body.

Tyrone's eyes widened and he pointed. "What the hell is that look!"

Dion wiped a hand over his face and stepped back from the car. "What look?"

Wesley's mouth lifted into a huge grin. "Oh, there definitely was a look. And there's something behind that smile."

Tyrone leaned out the window. "Forget the house, what happened after you two got back to her place?"

Minus specific details, Dion typically didn't mind talking to his brothers about the women he slept with. He and his brothers talked about the women they dated, the ones they liked and the ones they hoped to never see again. But he didn't want them to know he'd slept with Vanessa. They'd figure it out soon enough, because unless Vanessa was against it, he hoped to repeat the encounter. Multiple times. For now, he wanted to keep it to himself.

"Nothing happened," Dion said. "I helped her into the house, made sure she was okay, and then I was called into work."

"Okay, nothing happened," Tyrone said, not sounding convinced. "I've seen that goofy-ass grin on you before. Y'all slept together and you're feeling her."

Tyrone just had to be perceptive all the time. Dion could guess the reasons why his brother would tell him to leave her alone. He already knew the reasons. She was in town temporarily, she was a city girl, she had dreams much bigger than him and his small-town job.

"Just worry about getting the car for her, okay? I've got to get back to work."

Tyrone looked ready to push for more details, but Wesley shifted the car in gear. "Get back to work. We can talk more later."

Tyrone glanced at Wesley, who shook his head. With a sigh, Tyrone turned back to Dion. "Fine. Be safe out there, man."

He reached out the window. Dion bumped fists with his brother. "Always. Thanks again."

"We got you," Wesley said.

Dion stepped back and watched as his brothers drove off. He could imagine the grilling they'd give him later. He'd figure out how to answer them then. And control his facial expressions. He was feeling Vanessa. Way more than he should knowing this wasn't going anywhere.

He turned back toward the building. Right before he got to the door, he spotted his boss, Joe, walking out with Chad Gates, a guy who worked in the solid waste department and was also Joe's cousin. Chad and Joe laughed and slapped each other on the back as they came out of the building. Joe spotted Dion and his smile widened.

"Dion, just the man I was hoping to see. Did Amy call you?" Joe asked, referring to his administrative assistant. He was Dion's height with shifty blue eyes, and dark hair he combed over a balding spot. He hadn't come in the night before, but had shown up bright and early this morning to make sure Dion and the other crews were staying "on top of things."

Dion shook his head. "Not yet. What's up?"

"I'm setting up interviews for the division manager position." He wagged a finger at Dion. "You're the first on the list."

Dion blinked, surprised. He'd assumed he'd be interviewed because he was working as the interim superintendent. Many of the employees in the division already respected him and his decision-making skills. He hadn't expected Joe to say he was at the top of the list.

"Oh really?"

"Really," Joe said as if he'd given Dion some type of prize. He turned to Chad. "Dion is one of the best workers we've got. I wish I could have ten more men just like him."

Chad, who was shorter than his cousin and had shaved his head instead of trying to conceal the bald spot, gave Dion an assessing. "That's good to know."

Dion's brows drew together. That was odd. "I'm heading back to the garage now. We should have the rest of the trees cleared before three. I'll fill out the overtime forms tomorrow."

Joe waved a hand. "No rush on that. You come in late tomorrow since you've worked so hard this weekend. It's storm season, so I know you all will be busy."

"We're just trying to keep things going," Dion said.

"Good, good." Joe looked and nodded at Chad. "Well, we better get downtown." He turned back to Dion. "I've got to report on the road status to the administrator and council."

"I've already forwarded the status report for my crew to the emergency operations center." He'd done that because in the last storm Joe hadn't forwarded or read Dion's status report, which resulted in a miscommunication with the town leaders.

"I saw that. Good job, Dion." He slapped Dion on the shoulder. "Keep up the good work."

"Yeah, I will," Dion replied and watched as the two walked way.

Top of the list. Dion respected Joe as his supervisor more than he respected Joe as a person. The man was a micromanager who tended to panic and overreact in tough situations. Still, a small flicker of excitement stirred in his chest. Maybe Joe had noticed Dion's hard work and the promotion he wanted was just around the corner.

Vanessa reached for her phone only to realize for the hundredth time that morning that it wasn't there. She really was addicted to that thing. Someone knocked on her door before she could check the time and wonder when Dion would finally reach out to her.

She grinned as she opened the door and saw her grandmother. "What brings you here?"

"Dion called to tell me his brothers are picking up your car and bringing it to you. So I came over to give you an update."

Vanessa pressed a hand to her chest. "Good. I was hoping he wouldn't forget."

"Dion doesn't forget anything," Arletha said, settling down on the couch. She looked both comfortable and sassy in a burgundy velour jumpsuit.

Vanessa smiled at the defense in her grandmother's voice. "I get it, Grandma. He's a fine upstanding young man. I was worried because he was called in to work late yesterday afternoon. I wasn't sure if he'd have time to pick up my car."

"Called in to work or not, if he said he'd get it he would." Her grandmother crossed her legs and eyed Vanessa. "What I want to know is why your car is up there anyway."

Vanessa settled in the corner of the couch. She folded her legs beneath her and shrugged. "I wanted to see for myself. Without Dion and his brothers there with all their bells and whistles. If this place is so haunted like everyone says, then shouldn't I have felt something?"

Arletha tilted her head to the side. "Did you feel something?"

"I felt something on my foot." At her grandmother's

confused expression, Vanessa relayed the story of what happened the day before—ending with Dion bringing her home but leaving off the kiss and the sexy times afterward.

Arletha grunted, shook her head and gave Vanessa an I'm-disappointed-in-you look. "You know better than to go up there by yourself. What were you thinking? You could have been really hurt."

"I know, Grandma. I got an earful from Dion."

"You deserve an earful and a lot more," her grandmother continued to scold. "I don't care what kind of investigative reporter you're trying to be, putting yourself in an unsafe situation is not how you do that. Do you want to become the headline?"

Vanessa lowered her eyes. "No, ma'am."

"Okay, then. Next time you want to go check out a haunted house, take Dion with you or someone else. Don't go wandering into strange places alone anymore."

"I hear you. I promise I won't go wandering around strange places alone." She placed a hand over her heart. "I learned my lesson and will be feeling it for a while longer."

"How's your ankle and your leg?" her grandmother asked with concern now that the lecture was over.

"My ankle is stiff. I don't think it's sprained or anything. I had a cut on my leg and Dion put some ointment on it and a bandage."

Her grandmother's eyes narrowed. "He put some

ointment on it, huh?" A suspicious gleam lightened her eye.

Vanessa's cheeks heated. He'd done a lot more than tend to her wounded leg. That was one of the reasons she kept reaching for a phone that wasn't there. She wished she could blame the reflex on a social media addiction. Nope, she was obsessed with knowing when she'd get to see and talk to Dion again.

She glanced away from her grandmother to the television screen. "You ever watch this show? I don't usually get into survival shows but this one is about people being left in the wilderness for one hundred days or something."

"Mmm-hmm," her grandmother said, not looking at the television. "You wanna talk about this show instead of telling what else Dion tended to yesterday."

"Grandma!" Vanessa shifted uncomfortably underneath her grandmother's shrewd stare. "He helped me get home, that's all."

"Is that the reason why his truck was in your yard for about three hours yesterday? I started to come by, but I didn't want to interrupt the flow or see something I shouldn't."

Vanessa's jaw dropped. When her grandmother's smile spread, she snapped her mouth shut and held up a hand. "Oh my God, can we please not go there? I'm only in town for a short time. Don't get any ideas about me and Dion."

She didn't ask how her grandmother knew Dion's

truck was at her place for three hours. Sunshine Beach might be a tourist location, but it was still a small town. Locals knew each other and they stayed in each other's business. Half the town probably knew Dion had rescued her from her own clumsiness and spent three hours at her place helping her "recuperate."

The teasing light left Arletha's eye. "Be careful there, okay."

"Why? I thought you said Dion was a good guy."

Her grandmother nodded. "He is. He a great guy. Had his heart broken a while back and he hasn't really dated since then. A lot of women in town have their eye on him, but none caught his attention. You did. I know you don't want to stick around here long, so just, be careful. I like Dion. I don't want to see him get hurt while you get yourself together."

Vanessa was shocked into silence. She was being warned to be careful with Dion. "Shouldn't you be worried that he might hurt me?"

Her grandmother shook her head. "If Tyrone had caught your eye, maybe. But Dion isn't like his brother. He's looking for long term. If you're not, then you need to let him know up front."

The sound of multiple cars pulling into the yard kept Vanessa from responding. She glanced out the window behind the couch. Wesley pulled up in her rental while Tyrone followed in a larger vehicle.

"Is that the boys with your car?" Arletha asked.

Vanessa nodded. "That's them."

"Good. Be sure to thank them. They're such nice boys." Her grandmother got up and went to the door.

Vanessa followed at a slower pace. Her grandmother's words spun in her head. Dion was looking for long term. Was that really what he wanted? Something more than a quick fling? She hadn't considered that when she'd kissed him or when she'd invited him into the house. The thought filled her heart with unease. She wasn't staying in Sunshine Beach. She liked Dion, and wanted to sleep with him again, but she wasn't looking for a relationship. Not after the fiasco she'd gone through with her ex. Now was the time to focus on her, her career and her next moves. Not get caught up with a guy clearly tied to Sunshine Beach.

As she followed her grandmother outside and greeted Dion's brothers, she wondered if they also worried she'd hurt their brother. If she did, the entire town would believe she'd swept in, had her fun with the nice, eligible bachelor, then took off for bigger and better things. She didn't want that for Dion. She didn't want that for her. She had to make sure he understood they were just having fun. No longterm relationship required.

Chapter Nineteen

Vanessa's stomach growled like an angry wolf as she left the library at six that evening. She'd spent most of the day pulling up as much information as she could on the Bookersville house. There were dozens of articles about the place dating back decades. Mostly starting with the tragic death of the doctor who lived there and his wife who'd died from unusual circumstances.

The doctor's wife was poisoned. Because the doctor was having an affair with one of the nurses at the local hospital, many believed he poisoned her. He was acquitted of the murder due to lack of evidence, but, after he married the nurse, rumors spread of the doctor slowly losing his mind and claiming his late wife haunted their bedroom. He died of a broken neck after falling down the stairs. Stories spread the ghost of his wife pushed him.

Allegations circulated of an evil spirit upstairs and the ghost of the regretful husband downstairs. Each time the place was bought and sold, the legends resurfaced and eventually the house became a beacon for ghost investigators, supernatural enthusiasts and young kids looking for a quick thrill.

Vanessa sank deeper and deeper into fascination with each story. Several stories in the more recent years referenced Dion and his brothers. They had a following in the area that spread across the state and beyond. People sought them out for their opinions and knowledge. She was impressed.

She'd started the research believing that the stories would either give her insight or be campy and not have any substance. Except for a few silly pieces around Halloween each year, they mostly focused on the ghost's origin story and the people who experienced an encounter. The more she read, the more she understood that these people genuinely believed what they'd experienced was real and were shaken enough to seek people like Dion and his brothers to find answers.

The downside of being engrossed in research all day was forgetting to eat. She was ready to go to the first drive-through she could find and order the biggest size of any combo with a cookie on the side. Her cell phone rang just after she got in the car. Her heart flipped when she saw Dion's number. He hadn't called her all day, even though he had to have known his brothers had returned her phone. She hadn't wanted to admit it, especially after her grandmother's warning about being careful with Dion, but she'd worried he'd lost interest after they'd slept together.

"Hey, how's it going?" She cringed at the trying-hard-to-sound-nonchalant quality of her voice.

"I'm just getting off work and was hoping I could come by," his deep voice rumbled in her ear.

Vanessa's eyes jumped to the clock on her dash even though she knew it was after six. "You're just getting off work?"

"Yeah, I thought we'd wrap up sooner, but a sinkhole formed in one of the neighborhoods. We can't fix it today, but it took some time to block off the area and make it safe for the neighbors."

"Are you working tomorrow?"

"Bright and early at seven. We'll be working on that repair all day."

"You didn't get a weekend." He had to be tired, but he sounded upbeat.

"It's just this weekend. Plus, the overtime hours don't hurt. So, is it okay if I stop by?"

"I'm not at home, yet. I've been at the library all day. Thanks for asking your brothers to pick up my car and phone."

"No problem. I told you I'd get it. Even though I couldn't do it myself, I always deliver on my promises."

She was beginning to see that. "I still appreciate it. Were you coming now?" Her stomach growled. She needed to eat, but she was also eager to see him as soon as possible.

"I went home to shower and change. I was going to pick up something and bring it to you. That is, if you haven't eaten yet." His voice was a bit unsure.

Vanessa grinned. Not only did he want to come over, but he was bringing her food. The man was too good to be true. "I'll be home in about fifteen minutes, and I haven't eaten."

"You got a taste for anything?" Relief filled in his voice. She could almost imagine the smile on his handsome face.

"I've reached the stage of hungry where I'll eat almost anything, but I also have a taste for nothing."

Dion chuckled. The rich sound oozed through her car's Bluetooth speaker and wrapped around her like a cashmere cloak. "I know just the thing. You're good with seafood?"

"Anything except oysters. I don't like them."

"She doesn't like oysters. I've got you. See you in about…thirty minutes?"

She grinned. That gave her just enough time to go home and freshen up. Even though she'd just sat in a library all day, she was wrinkled and still wearing the lounge clothes she'd had on when his brothers dropped off her car. "That's perfect."

"Good. Can't wait to see you."

* * *

The doorbell rang just after Vanessa jumped out of the shower and dressed in a pair of leggings and an oversize sweatshirt. Her heart jumped and she had to fight back a grin. She hurried to the door but caught a glimpse of herself in the hallway mirror. She snatched the plastic shower cap off her head and stuffed it behind the decorative sailboat on the half table in the hallway before rushing to the door.

She smoothed back the damp edges of her hair, took a deep breath to calm her heart and opened the door.

Dion's full lips lifted in a crooked smile that warmed her better than the hot shower she'd taken. "Hey, I brought food."

"Then you're allowed to enter." She stepped back. "I think my stomach is about to revolt if I don't feed it soon."

Dion walked through the door. "We can't have that happening."

He took up so much space in the small hallway. His broad shoulders and chest filled out the thin, dark orange sweater he wore. His long legs and per- fectly rounded ass looked even more tempting in his dark jeans. Her eyes dropped to his biceps and she remembered how he'd torn away the piece of wood sticking into her leg. Delicious tingles rippled across her skin.

"Where you want me to put the food?"

Vanessa jerked her eyes up from their appraisal

of his many assets. His crooked smile increased, and a knowing spark lit his eye. Her cheeks burned but she only raised a brow. Yeah, she was checking him out and thinking about the night before. If she wasn't so hungry, she would've said skip the food and jumped into his arms.

"The kitchen is fine."

He nodded and headed in that direction. Vanessa followed and the savory aroma of fried food drifted to her nostrils. She temporarily forgot about how much she wanted to be in Dion's arms as another hunger took over.

"What did you get?"

Dion set the plastic bag with take-out containers on the table. "I went by the seafood place near my house. They have a shrimp basket special on Sundays. It's one of my favorites especially after I've worked on the weekend."

Vanessa's mouth watered even more. She opened one of the containers to find it overflowing with baby shrimp, fries and hushpuppies. "It's almost obscene the amount of food in this container."

"You'll definitely get two meals out of this." Dion reached into the bag and pulled out containers filled with tartar sauce, cocktail sauce and ketchup.

"As hungry as I am now, I could probably eat the entire container in one sitting." Vanessa grabbed a tartar sauce and ketchup.

Dion chuckled. "Don't do that. I've done it before

and while it was good going down, my stomach felt like it was going to explode."

"I'm almost tempted to threaten stomach explosion. I've got water, tea and soda." She walked to the fridge and opened it.

"Tea."

"Good choice." Vanessa pulled out a gallon jug of tea and grabbed two plastic cups out of the bag on the counter and went back to the table.

They settled at the table, and for several minutes only the sound of them eating, interrupted by their occasional grunts of enjoyment, filled her kitchen. Vanessa enjoyed every morsel and it wasn't just because she was so hungry. She enjoyed having Dion there with her. Watching him enjoy his food instead of going through a long diatribe about how fried food was terrible and lamenting about the two-day juice cleanse they'd have to go on just to make up for eating poorly for one meal. Something her ex would have talked about the entire time they ate.

Vanessa sat back and took a deep breath. She splayed her hand across her stomach. "Oh my goodness that was so good. I feel like I need to catch my breath."

Dion grinned and leaned back in his chair. "I feel you." He glanced at her half-eaten container of food. "I thought you were going to eat everything."

"I almost did, but you were right. My stomach told me to stop. Thank you for bringing dinner. I got so caught up in my work I forgot to eat."

He closed the carton on his food and pushed it aside. "What were you doing at the library?"

"Looking up the history on that house."

His eyes widened. "Really? What made you do that?"

"I wanted to know more about the land, the people who lived there, why so many people think the place is haunted."

"And what did you find out?"

She leaned her arms on the table. "I was fascinated," she admitted.

"What fascinated you?"

"The story of the original family for starters. That's a whole bunch of drama. Then everything that happened afterward. The people who've experienced something there."

"Do you believe in ghosts now?"

Vanessa held up a hand. "I'm not saying all of that, but I do believe the people who've been there believe something happened. Whatever happened moved them enough to seek answers. You and your brothers are never condescending or deceitful. You guys have helped a lot of people."

His brows rose. "You investigated me and my brothers and not just the house?" He didn't sound offended, just surprised.

"Once I started it was easy to go down the rabbit hole of the three brothers who investigate ghosts in the area. I expected you to find evidence of ghosts at every home you went to, but that isn't the case."

He shook his head. "Our goal isn't to prove every place is haunted. That's why we investigate. Sometimes the flickering lights and cold rooms are just bad wiring and weird air circulation. We want to find out the truth and ease people's fears."

"I'll admit I jumped to conclusions when my grandmother first mentioned you helping her. I was worried she'd be taken advantage of. But if you all can give her some peace, then I'm okay with that."

Dion's spine straightened and he smiled just enough to bring out his dimples. "Does that mean you're going to let us investigate her house?"

She moved her head side to side and glanced at the sky. "I guess so."

"And what about the pilot for the show?"

"That's for grandma to decide." She'd butted in enough for now.

"I think she's good, but I'll double-check. Tyrone is excited about it. He wants to spotlight your grandmother's house because she's such a well-known person in the community. She's always believed in us."

The awe in his voice caught her attention. "Do you believe in you?"

He glanced away and toyed with the edge of his to-go box. "What do you mean?"

"Do you believe in what you and your brothers are trying to do? To turn your side hustle investigating ghosts into a television show?"

He shrugged his large shoulders. "I don't know what to believe. I know Tyrone thinks we have a chance and I'm good with supporting him. I'm concentrating on more realistic dreams right now."

"Dion, I may not believe in ghosts, but a producer wants to film a pilot. I think your dream is pretty realistic."

"Wanting to film a pilot and actually getting a show are two different things. I've never had big dreams of becoming famous. I'm happy here. I like my job and I'm up for a promotion at work. My interview is Wednesday. I think I've got a good shot." He shifted in his seat, his body stiff.

She was making him uncomfortable. He seemed so confident and sure in all their interactions before that seeing him showing doubt was surprising. Words of encouragement and don't suppress your big dreams bubbled up in her throat. She reminded herself that this thing with Dion was temporary. They weren't in a relationship. She shouldn't stick her nose where it didn't belong.

"I hope you get the job," she said with a smile.

The tension in his shoulders eased. "So do I. I know it's not as big as the television thing, and if that were to work out, I'd do it for my brothers."

"What's your big dream?" Did he want anything for himself and not just his brothers?

"To be settled and secure. After my parents died, everything was hectic and crazy. I took the job with the town, stepped up so Wes and Tyrone would know they could count on me. Now, I just want to help people, keep working and one day get married and start a family. It's old-fashioned and simple, but that's the kind of guy I am."

A bittersweet squeeze tightened her heart. His dream was simple but that didn't make it any less sweet. Her grandmother's warning came back. Dion wanted the same things she wanted, but in a vastly different way. While she loved Sunshine Beach and being close to her grandmother, she loved being a reporter at a large station in a large city even more. She liked the excitement and vibe of being surrounded by so many people and so many opportunities.

"Too small, huh?" he asked in a self-deprecating voice.

She shook her head. "No, it's perfect."

"What about you? Was being a reporter always your goal?"

She rested her elbow on the table and propped her head in her hand. "It was. My dad was a newspaper reporter. He would come home talking about the stories he worked on, the corruption he'd uncover and the needs of people whose voices weren't typically heard. I wanted to be like him. When he died, I made a promise to carry on his legacy. When I got the job at the station in Atlanta, it was a dream come true. Even though he wasn't there, I felt my dad's pride."

She sighed and scraped her nail on the table. She'd thought she was following in her father's footsteps. Instead, the station didn't think she had what it took.

Dion's hand covered hers. She looked up and he

squeezed her hand. "Look what you did today. You took your curiosity about the house and spent the day finding out the truth. Another station will see you're just as hard hitting as the next person."

"You don't think I'm too cute or too bubbly?" she asked, repeating the phrases that had come out when she was fired.

"Cute? Woman, you are fine as hell," he said, eyeing her from head to toe. Vanessa laughed and tried to pull away, but he held on to her hand. "That doesn't mean you aren't smart, tenacious and driven. You don't have to be one or the other."

The squeeze around her heart tightened. She was falling for him. That wasn't supposed to happen. They'd slept together and they'd come to a truce about her grandmother's home, but this couldn't be anything more than a friends-with-benefits type arrangement. She had to get herself together before she forgot that Sunshine Beach was just a pit stop on her way to her future.

"You're right," she said brightly and pulled her hand back. "Another station will realize that soon enough and I'll be moving on to a bigger and better job. You'll get your promotion and have your stability. And—" she held up a finger "—you'll get the television show and become a superstar."

The light in his eyes dimmed for a second before he took a deep breath and nodded. Maybe he also had to remind himself they had dreams separate from each other.

Chapter Twenty

"Wait, are you for real? Vanessa is going to let us investigate her grandmother's house?" Tyrone's disbelieving voice echoed against the metal walls of the shed in Dion's backyard.

He'd texted his brothers earlier in the day with the good news. He'd expected them to be excited about the opportunity. He hadn't expected them to show up at his place after work to ask fifty-'leven questions about how he'd convinced her. His plan was to spend the afternoon working on a replacement screen door for his back porch, not entertain his brothers.

He should have known they'd show up. He still lived in the house they'd stayed in when his parents died. It was their connection to their parents and still the place they came together to discuss major decisions, hang out or just recharge after a bad day.

"Yes," Dion said. "She agreed yesterday. When do you want to do it?" Dion marked the spots on the two-by-four where he'd cut it for the doorframe.

Wes, who sat on a stool next to the pool table, answered. "I say we do it this weekend. Before she changes her mind."

Tyrone leaned against the opposite side of the pool table and shook his head. "We can't that soon. I need to get in contact with Tiana. She's excited about us, but she had to move on to another job when we got sidelined by Vanessa."

Tyrone's voice still held lingering resentment. Dion understood. Tyrone wanted the television show the most. He'd always had big dreams of being more than a kid from a small Southern town. He wanted the bright lights that came with a life in show business.

"Then find out when she can come," Dion said. "Then I'll get with Vanessa and Mrs. Montgomery and let them know when we plan to investigate."

"Are you sure she won't change her mind?" Tyrone asked with a skeptical frown on his face. "I mean she was dead set against us and thought we were using her grandmother."

"That was before she went to the Bookersville house," Dion explained. "She spent the next day researching the history of the place and the encounters people had."

Wes spun the barstool from side to side. "Does she believe now?"

Dion shook his head. "Not exactly. She accepts people are looking for answers for the things they encounter. She respects that we try to help people find answers. She admitted she initially believed we were willing to go along with anyone who thought they had a spirit in their home as long as we got paid. Now she realizes there's more to that."

Tyrone's chest puffed up. "We wouldn't do that to anyone."

"I know that. Mrs. Montgomery knows that, but Vanessa didn't. She had to get to know us. Now she trusts us not to take advantage of her grandmother."

Wesley cocked a brow. "Your truck being at her house all last night have anything to do with that?"

Dion's face heated. "Who said my truck was there all night?" He didn't look up as he focused on cutting the two-by-four with his table saw.

Wesley laughed. "Don't even try to front like you weren't there. This town is small enough for regulars to know when a local's car is parked at a visitor's house. You were there."

Tyrone braced his hands on the pool table and eyed Dion with interest. "I hadn't heard this bit of news. I thought you and Vanessa were just friends. You spending the night now?"

"It's not like that."

Wesley cocked his head to the side. "Then tell us

what it's like. Because you don't usually get caught slipping like that."

Dion held up his hand in surrender. "Look, for real, nothing happened."

Tyrone gave him a cut-the-crap smirk. "You expect me to believe you spent the entire night at Vanessa's place and nothing happened? Bruh, you think we haven't noticed the way you two are around each other. If you got a little bit, that's fine. You don't have to be embarrassed. It's about time."

"I didn't get anything last night," Dion said. His brothers exchanged looks as if they were disappointed. Dion's face heated up even more. He hated to reveal the truth, because that was more embarrassing than the hell he'd catch once his brothers knew he'd slept with Vanessa.

Wes turned to Tyrone. "You know what, maybe he just slept on the couch all night."

Dion rubbed the back of his head. "I did."

Tyrone's eyes narrowed. "Did what?"

Dion nodded and let out a heavy sigh. "I stopped by to check on her after what happened the day before. We ate some food, then sat on the couch to watch TV, and then…"

Wesley leaned in closer. "And then what?"

"And then I fell asleep. Right there on the damn couch. I woke up at four in the morning with a blanket tossed over me and a crook in my damn neck."

Silence followed his admission. Tyrone and Wesley exchanged looks. A beat later, they both started laughing.

"You playing?" Wesley said.

Dion rubbed his temple. "I wish I were. She didn't wake me up or anything. Just threw a blanket on me and let me sleep."

He hadn't called Vanessa today because he was embarrassed. Going to bed early and falling asleep after working overtime were things that had bugged the hell out of his ex. Examples she'd used about why he was boring or acting like an old man.

He hadn't meant to fall asleep. His plan was to show up, woo Vanessa with good food and then work their way into repeating what happened the day before. Except, when she'd asked if he wanted to watch television after they ate, he'd agreed. But somewhere between her soft warm curves against his side and a baking competition show, he'd fallen asleep. He couldn't bear to see her disappointment or, worse disgust after he'd conked out like the old man his ex claimed he was.

"You fell asleep?" Tyrone asked as if he didn't understand the idea of falling asleep.

"I did."

"And she just left you on the couch?" Tyrone said in a flat voice.

"What did you want her to do? Wake me up and toss me out?" Dion asked.

Wesley cut in before Tyrone could question him. "What did she say when you woke up?"

"Nothing," Dion said. "She made coffee and asked if I wanted to get breakfast at Waffle House."

"Did you go?" Tyrone asked.

"Nah, I left and went home to get ready for work."

Tyrone looked as if he wanted to shake him. "Why didn't you go to breakfast with her?"

"Because I fell asleep on her couch. She was just being nice. I figured I wouldn't overextend my welcome and left."

Tyrone walked over and placed a hand on Dion's shoulder. "If she wanted you to go, she wouldn't have asked you about breakfast. She wouldn't have made you coffee. She would have just kicked you out and that would be the end of it."

Wesley rubbed his chin and eyed Dion. "What's up with you two anyway? I mean, you saved her from the Bookersville house, made us get her car and brought her food. Now you're sleeping on her couch. Are you two...dating?"

He wasn't exactly sure what they were doing. He only knew he wasn't ready for her to give him the same disgusted, I-can-do-better-than-you look he'd gotten previously. "We're just cool. That's all."

"Because you know she's only in town for a little while," Wesley said.

Tyrone's hand tightened on Dion's shoulder. "That's what makes this perfect. Dion is looking for a woman to settle down with and make some babies. Vanessa is not that woman, but that doesn't mean he can't rebound with her."

Dion knocked away his brother's hand. "Rebound? I'm not rebounding."

"You've barely dated since Keisha left. Have fun with Vanessa, and since you know she's leaving, you don't have to worry about where things are going. Dust off your old moves and once she leaves maybe you'll be ready to start dating again."

"That's not what this is," Dion said.

"Why not? You think Vanessa is looking for a relationship? She's here because her man dumped her, and she lost a job. You're both doing the other a favor with no strings attached."

He didn't like it, but Tyrone's words resonated. Vanessa was eventually leaving. She didn't expect more from him so he didn't have to worry about her eventually seeing him as a boring, small-town guy with no vision. He'd noticed the look on her face when he'd downplayed the idea of getting a show because he'd seen it before. The look that would eventually make her seek out someone else.

"Let's not talk about me and Vanessa. Right now we're cool. Just friends. I fell asleep on her couch, and she was kind enough to let me stay. That's it."

"Dion—"

He cut off Tyrone's argument. "For real. I'm not putting a lot of stock in anything happening with us. I'm more concerned about my interview on Wednesday."

Tyrone turned away. "You and that damn job."

Dion's stance shifted and he glared. "What about me and that damn job?"

"They don't appreciate you, Dion. You can do better."

"And I suppose you think this television show is better."

"It is. Much better than sucking up to that supervisor of yours."

Dion took a long breath. He wasn't going to argue about this again. "Look, the television show is your dream. Not mine. I'm willing to help you because you're my brother and I support you. All I'm asking is for you to do the same. I've worked hard and I've been with the city for seventeen years. This is the next step for me."

Tyrone threw up his hands. "Fine. You wanna be stuck in that nowhere position with people who don't appreciate you, that's on you. When this television show works out, you'll finally see that you're worth a lot more."

"I already know what I'm worth."

Wesley jumped up from the barstool and held up his hand. "Whoa, hold up. There's nothing wrong with what either of you want, and you know that." He looked at Dion. "But, man, you know they're not always loyal at the town. You can want both."

"What?" Dion asked, affronted.

"The promotion and the show," Wesley replied. "It's okay to want them both."

Dion turned away from him and picked up another two-by-four. "Now you're sounding like Tyrone."

"That's because he's right."

Tyrone slapped his chest. "See."

Wesley pushed Tyrone's shoulder. "Shut up." He looked back at Dion. "You gave up a lot when Mom and Dad died. We appreciate that, but you don't have to keep giving up the things you want. That's all I'm saying. We're good. You can want both."

Dion glanced at his brothers. He expected censure or frustration in their eyes. Instead, he saw compassion. Not once had he ever complained about giving up the college scholarship, taking the first job he could get, becoming a father figure when he was barely out of high school. He'd done that for his brothers. He knew they appreciated it. He even knew Tyrone gave him a hard time because he wanted the best for him.

He knew that, but he still held back. He wasn't ready to admit to them the fear in his heart. The fear of having something he wanted snatched away.

Clearing his throat, he grabbed the tape measure. "Let's get through Mrs. Montgomery's investigation and then we'll worry about what I want."

Chapter Twenty-One

Vanessa's cell phone rang while she sat in the middle of the living room floor surrounded by printouts of articles, blog posts and property records related to hauntings investigated by Dion and his brothers. She smiled, seeing her sister's number on the screen and answered.

"Hey, lady, what's up?"

"That's why I'm calling you," Jada said in her customary bold tone. "What's this Momma talking about a ghost at Grandma's?"

Vanessa shook her head even though her sister couldn't see her. "Girl, you sound like me when I first got here."

"What is going on? Grandpa really haunting her?"

Vanessa sighed. "Well, we're trying to find out."

Vanessa spent the next few minutes updating Jada about their grandmother's concerns and her plan to hire Dion and his brothers to investigate. Surprisingly, Jada wasn't against the idea and wanted to know more about the brothers. As her sister pushed for more information, Vanessa admitted what happened between her and Dion.

She had to. Not talking about what was, or wasn't, going on with them was driving her up the wall. Even though she liked Sheri, she wasn't ready to unload her insecurities about sleeping with Dion to her. He'd rescued her, literally swept her off her feet, then blew her back out with amazing sex. Not only that, but he'd also arranged her car delivery and brought her food. She'd thought they were vibing. Instead, he'd disappeared quickly the next morning, and hadn't called her.

"I shouldn't care, should I? I shouldn't call him, either, right?"

"Vanessa, what do we always say about guys?" her sister said, sounding like a teacher repeating a lesson to her class.

Vanessa pinched the bridge of her nose. "Be direct and ask what's up instead of pretending we're mind readers."

"Exactly. If you really like the guy, ask him what's up. If this is just a fling to get over Daniel, then forget him."

"It's not just a fling," Vanessa said. She'd known

she and Daniel were over the second she'd left Atlanta for Sunshine Beach. She'd been hurt that he'd used a horoscope to break up with her, then angry when she realized that was an excuse to start dating other people. That didn't mean she was ready to admit that she *like* liked Dion.

"Okay, then call him and find out what's going on."

"It's not that easy." Vanessa fell back on the floor and stared at the ceiling. "Isn't this too soon for me to like a new guy? Shouldn't I not care? Shouldn't I make this just a fling?"

"Says who? Seriously, Vanessa, I need you to get out of your own head. Who says you have to do relationships a certain way? I told you plenty of times to get rid of Daniel. He didn't deserve you. He let his horoscope give him a reason to dump you the day you were fired. Now he's seeing someone else. Do you really think he's sitting around worried about if he's moved on too soon?"

"No," Vanessa said with an eye roll. She doubted he'd given her and their relationship a second thought.

"So why are you putting some random statute of limitations on when you can start feeling another guy? You left Atlanta and went to Sunshine Beach to find yourself, discover what you really want and not settle for less. You don't have to feel sorry about being into this Dion guy if he makes you happy."

"But I'm only here for a short time. I'm looking for a job elsewhere."

"As you should. I'm not telling you to give up your career for him, but not being in the same city as someone isn't an automatic killer of relationships. Find out what's going on with him and if things progress, cool. If they don't, well, at least you had decent sex before you moved on."

Vanessa burst out laughing. "You are a fool."

"No, I'm your sister and I have to kick you in the ass with the truth every once in a while." Jada's voice was firm but caring.

"You do and that's why I love you. You're right. I need to talk to him. Even if he says he's not interested."

"And if he does, then forget him."

Easier said than done. Vanessa didn't think she'd easily forget Dion even after she left town. "I at least need to know what's going on."

"I bet you he's sitting at his place waiting on you to call."

Vanessa's head tilted to the side. She hadn't considered that because, as her sister said, she'd been all in her head. She hadn't realized how much her previous relationship was still screwing with her thinking. Ever since a horoscope was enough to convince Daniel, a man she'd dated for a year, to break up with her, she'd accepted that she lacked something, some spark, that would make her more important than a prediction. Between that and getting fired, she was about to sink into a place she may have stayed for a long time if her sister hadn't snapped her out of it.

"Thank you," she said.

"Anytime." Vanessa could hear the smile in Jada's voice. "That's what big sisters are for."

Even after her sister's pep talk, Vanessa hesitated to call Dion. She alternated between "why hasn't he called me?" suspicion to "why in the world wouldn't he call me?" ferocity. She decided to give him until after his interview before she searched him out and confronted him. Though she knew she hesitated because she wasn't ready to face another rejection.

When Wednesday came with still no word from Dion, she drove to the store on his side of town to pick up a few things. The idea of dropping by to see him crossed her mind as she left the store. Not just because her body couldn't forget the way he'd touched her, but because she wanted to see him. She needed answers.

She sat in the car in the parking lot and pulled her cell phone out of her purse. She'd just call him. If anything, he needed to talk to her about investigating her grandmother's home. When she'd asked her grandmother earlier if she'd heard from Dion or his brothers about setting a date, her grandmother hadn't.

She pulled up Dion's number and her finger hovered over the green call icon. Her cell phone rang. She jumped at the sudden surprise, then her eyes widened after Dion's name flashed on the screen.

Her hand tightened around the phone and she didn't care about the grin splitting her face.

She cleared her throat, swiped the answer icon, pressed a hand to her chest and tried not to sound overly eager as she answered. "Dion? Hey, what's up?"

"Hey, Vanessa. What are you up to?" Other than the slight hesitation in his greeting, Dion's voice came through calm and unbothered.

"I'm just leaving the grocery store. I needed to pick up a few things." She cringed and slapped her forehead. Duh, why else would she be at the store.

"Oh, I just got off work and was heading home."

She waited for him to say more. Why hadn't he called? How had his interview gone? Did he want her to stop by?

"I was thinking about you and decided to give you a call." He sounded shy and sweet, and affection squeezed her heart in a huge bear hug.

"I'm near your side of town. I could drop by if you're not doing anything after work." She said the words quickly. Before she could rethink her decision.

"That's cool. You know the address?"

Her grin returned. "Text it to me."

"Alright. See you in a bit."

Vanessa ended the call and did a quick happy dance in her seat. Then she took a calming breath. This still didn't explain the reason why he had taken off without looking at her and hadn't called for two days. She would get the answer for that before anything else.

Dion texted her his address, followed by another text saying he would be in his shed in the back. She put his address in her car's navigation system and headed that way. Dion lived in a beautiful two-story, colonial-style home on a spacious lot. The house was painted a light blue color with black shutters and the yard was neat and well kept, with large shade trees and trimmed hedges. Not surprising knowing Dion, without any extras like flowers or fall decorations like some of the other houses in the area. She pulled in behind his work truck parked next to his personal gray truck.

The shed, as he called it, looked more like a split-level garage. The lights were on and the door open. Vanessa crossed the grass to the open door. The interior of the shed was just as neat as the yard. One side held a work area with tools. The other side a pool table, television and mini fridge. Dion stood in the work area and examined the wall.

Vanessa knocked and Dion turned and faced her. Her breath caught. She'd had enough mental images of Dion looking sexy in his work uniform, a casual T-shirt and shirtless to last her a lifetime. She was not prepared for Dion in a suit. Broad shoulders filled the dark blue jacket, and the white shirt beneath was opened at the neck with the tie loosened. Vanessa had a strong urge to grab the tie, pull him forward and press her lips against his.

"You clean up nice," was all she could say.

He gave a shy smile that made her want to pinch his dimpled cheeks before shoving him against a wall and kissing him. "Thanks. I had the interview today."

"I remember. How did it go?"

He lifted a shoulder. "I don't know. You can never tell with these things. I answered all the questions, gave my thoughts on ways to improve our section, I even surprised him with my background."

Vanessa came farther into the shed and leaned her hip against the pool table. "How was he surprised? You've worked there for years."

"I have, but he's only been the deputy director for two. He knew I gave up a scholarship for my brothers, but didn't know I went to school online a few years ago to get a degree in political science with a minor in business. He also didn't know I'd taken a few leadership courses the town offered."

"What did he say after he found out?"

Dion walked over and stood next to her. "He was surprised, but also kind of… I don't know. He didn't say anything specifically, but his level of surprise threw me. As if he hadn't imagined that I would have a degree or know anything other than how to patch a pothole or run a chain saw. It was kind of insulting."

Vanessa nodded in understanding. "Yeah, that whole underestimate you just because they don't bother to see past the surface."

"Yeah, that didn't sit right with me. Kind of put me in a weird space for the rest of the interview."

"When they fired me at the station because I didn't fit their investigative goals, I pointed out how the stories I worked on may have seemed like fluff to them, but I did the hard work to investigate and give a new take that always received good feedback. I remember my boss looking as if I'd hit him upside the head with a brick. He couldn't imagine taking the skills I'd learned where I was and using them somewhere else. That's when I knew he'd never see me for what I can do."

He crossed his arms and leaned against the table next to her. "I was thinking the same thing today."

Vanessa frowned. "You want to leave?"

He shrugged again. "I'm not saying all that. Just thinking about what my brothers said. That I shouldn't settle. Maybe I'm overthinking. I'll wait until they make their decision."

"Hey, let's go with he was so impressed with you that it's even more obvious why the person everyone already thought was getting the job should get the job."

He chuckled and nodded. "Let's go with that."

She glanced around. "Why are you out here still in your suit?"

"Wesley needed to borrow my drill. I came to make sure that's all he borrowed."

"Does he take your stuff?"

Dion nodded. "Wesley is a tech guy, but not a hand tool guy. Which means he views my tools as his tools. He took the drill, but also my screwdriver set. If I don't double-check, that set will stay at his place."

"Baby brothers, what you gonna do?" she said with a teasing smile.

"Get my stuff back. That's what." His smile softened and he slid closer. "Hey, sorry for not calling all week."

Vanessa's lips parted on her sharp inhale. She planned to broach the subject, but he'd surprised her by apologizing.

"I assumed you realized you weren't that into me." She tried to keep her voice light to try to hide how much his not calling had bothered her, but some of her frustration crept in.

Dion took her hand in his. "First I was embarrassed."

She frowned. "About what?"

"Falling asleep on your couch like that. I go to bed early. It had been a long weekend cleaning up after the storm. We got behind on the regular work and have been playing catch-up all week. When I get off, I eat and fall out."

"That's no reason to be embarrassed."

"I know that up here." He pressed a finger to his head. "But I've also been told my early-to-bed, early-to-rise lifestyle is boring. I didn't want you to think I was some old man who couldn't hang."

Vanessa shook her head. "Why would I? I had to be at the station at three for the morning show. I'm in bed by eight some nights and still wake up at three in the morning. I get it."

He sighed and looked relieved. "I should have

called. I'm still sorry for that. The days were busy. Yeah, there were times in between when I could have called or texted, but well, I haven't dated in a while."

"Dated?" Vanessa's heart picked up.

He grinned and tugged on her hand. "Don't look like that. Yes, dated. I know you're here temporarily. I know you're leaving. I don't care about any of that right now. While you're here, I'd like to be the man you're with. I don't sleep around, and I don't play games. When you leave, we'll deal with that, but until then, know that I'm not seeing anyone else, calling anyone else or sleeping with anyone but you."

That was her clue to clear things up. She should say they were hooking up while she was in town but weren't dating. She should make sure he understood there wasn't room for long-term expectations with what they were doing. When she got a job offer, she was out of Sunshine Beach without a backward glance. He should protect his heart.

The words refused to form. Instead of doing what she should do, she went with what she wanted to do since she'd seen him in that suit. She grabbed his tie and pulled him closer. "I never once thought you couldn't hang and please believe me when I say that if I find out you're giving it to anyone one else while I'm here, I will castrate you."

Dion flinched, then raised a brow. "You really gotta go there?"

She shrugged. "Just letting you know." She reached between them and cupped his growing hardness in her hand. "I'm the only one who gets this." She gently squeezed, then ran her palm up and down his length.

He lifted her quickly and easily onto the pool table. Vanessa gasped and clasped his shoulders. Dion's devilish grin made her sex clench.

"You're about to get something."

Chapter Twenty-Two

Dion's alarm clock went off at 4:00 a.m. Typically, he groaned, turned it off and frowned as his mind immediately filled with all the tasks waiting for him at work. This morning, he grinned and reached over in the bed as his mind filled with all the ways he'd made love to Vanessa the night before.

His hand met empty sheets. Frowning, he sat up quickly. Even in the darkness of the room he could tell she wasn't there. Had she left while he slept? He knew mentioning the word *dating* had given her a moment of panic. He understood she didn't want him thinking this was going anywhere serious. He knew she was on the rebound and she wasn't in town for long. He was guarding his heart very closely, but he would make it clear that he wasn't into the hit-and-dip routine. No more misunderstandings in this relationship even if it was short term.

He threw back the covers and stood when the smell of coffee drifted into the room. He went to the bedroom door and the sound of the television drifted down the hall. He walked to the kitchen and spotted Vanessa, wearing nothing but the long tunic shirt she'd had on the night before. Relief and joy swept through him. He leaned against the wall and watched as she scrolled through her phone and poured coffee. Guess she hadn't lied about waking up at 3:00 a.m.

He liked having her there in his kitchen. Liked seeing her hair wild after she'd said it was going to be a mess without her head wrap once he'd convinced her to sleep over instead of driving back home. Liked watching her pull her lower lip between her teeth and laugh at something on the screen of her phone. Liked the way she seemed at ease in his space as if she belonged there.

The last made him straighten. No thoughts of belonging. He'd seen the look in her eye the night before. She may have agreed to them being exclusively together while she was in town, but he couldn't forget the most important part. While she was in town. He'd better remember that before he got any ideas about them being anything more than friends with benefits.

Don't get attached.

He knocked on the wall to get her attention and

to avoid startling her since she was looking at the phone.

She glanced up at him and grinned. Her smile so bright and sexy the reminder to not get attached was blasted away. "Hey, did I wake you up?"

He shook his head and came farther into the kitchen. "My alarm went off. How long have you been up?"

"About thirty minutes. I couldn't sleep anymore and decided to watch television."

Dion stood in front of her and rested his hands on the counter on either side of her. "You could have woken me up."

Her eyes warmed and her body softened. "I didn't want to disturb you. You've had a busy week, so I decided to let you sleep in."

Dion leaned forward and pressed a kiss to her neck. She smelled so damn good. "For the record, you can wake me up early any time you wish."

She put her coffee mug down on the counter and wrapped her arms around his waist. Her head tilted to the side, giving him better access to her neck. "Wake you up to exercise or to watch the morning news with me?"

"Whatever you want to wake me up for. As long as I'm seeing your face in the morning."

Dion realized the words implied a commitment. He started to pull back, pretend as if he wasn't having thoughts about her belonging or feelings of attachment, except her body trembled and she held on to him tighter.

"I'm starting to think you're the real smooth talker of the family."

He relaxed and continued to kiss up her neck to her ear. "Not a smooth talker. Just a guy who speaks the truth."

"Mmm," she moaned and clutched his waist. "I thought about making breakfast."

"You don't have to make breakfast."

"Good, because I'm not good at making breakfast. I'm a passable cook, but my pancakes aren't winning any contests."

Dion chuckled and ran a hand beneath her tunic. Her skin was soft and warm against his palm. He took one full breast in his hand and gently squeezed. "I don't give a damn about pancakes." His thumb brushed over her hardening nipple.

"I…can scramble a decent egg." Her voice trembled.

Dion nudged his thigh between her leg. "Why are you insisting on making breakfast?"

"Because, you have to get ready for work so I'm trying to be helpful."

Dion leaned back and smiled. "Just seeing you here is helpful." Helpful and something he could get used to.

Her eyes got that look from the night before. The "Are we getting too close?" look. He wasn't ready to face that right now. He lifted her onto the counter, and she gasped. Her legs spread and she bit her lower lip.

"Who needs eggs," he said before crouching between her thighs.

* * *

Dion and Vanessa walked through the doors of the Waffle House an hour later. He was well aware showing up with Vanessa would get the gossip tongues wagging, but he didn't care. He meant what he'd said. While Vanessa was in town, he was with her. He wasn't ashamed of that.

The workers from the town were in their usual spot. They waved and called him over when he entered. Dion shook his head and led Vanessa to a booth on the opposite side of the diner. There was some good-natured "Oh it's like that now" and "You're ditching us this morning, huh?" after he and Vanessa were seated.

Sheri came over with two cups and the pot of coffee. "Good morning, you two. Your usual?" She eyed them with a sly grin but thankfully didn't comment on them arriving together.

Vanessa nodded. "The usual for me."

"Same," Dion agreed.

Sheri's grin widened as she poured the coffee. "Coming right up." She winked at Vanessa, who blushed and glanced away, before walking away to call in their order.

"Everyone is going to know I spent the night at your place now, right?" Vanessa said.

"Everyone already knows I spent the night at your place over the weekend. Is that a problem?" He didn't feel the need to hide their relationship from others, but he wasn't sure about Vanessa. She lived in Atlanta, where her personal life wouldn't be known by everyone in the vicinity overnight. She may not like or want to deal with the small-town gossip.

She shrugged. "It's not a problem for me. I'm just worried about you."

"Why would you be worried about me?"

"Well… What about when I leave?"

He reached over and took her hand in his. "I'm not worried about when you leave or what people will say afterward. I'm a grown man and you're a grown woman. What we do while you're here is our business."

She studied him for a second, concern and hesitancy clear in her beautiful brown eyes. She sighed and nodded. "You're right. I'm just… I don't want people to think I'm using you."

He raised a brow. "Are you using me?"

She shook her head. "No!"

"Then who cares what they think. I knew what I was getting into. You just got out of a relationship. You're looking at having to do a career change. You're only in town until you get your life together. I understand I'm just a small part of that equation."

He said the words with a nonchalant shrug even though his throat wanted to close up. He tried to channel Tyrone's words. They were both getting something out of this. He didn't need to feel wrong or upset about the truth of their situation.

A small line formed between her brows. She opened her mouth, but Sheri came over with his toast, grits and bacon. "Here you go. I'll be right back with your waffles and bacon, Vanessa."

Vanessa gave Sheri a small smile. "Thank you."

Dion didn't look at Vanessa as he smeared grape jelly on his toast. He didn't want to revisit their previous conversation. All his big words about understanding he was just a pit stop on her path toward a better life didn't have the effect he'd hoped. He'd hoped to reassure her he wasn't going to get too attached or overly involved while they were together. Instead, speaking the words out loud only made him yearn for something he couldn't quite articulate exactly.

"What's on your agenda for today?" he said before she could bring up the conversation again.

She gave him a look as if she wanted to discuss them more, but Sheri returned with Vanessa's food. After she dropped off the waffles, bacon and hot syrup, she walked away, and Vanessa answered his question.

"I got a text from one of my friends at the station in Atlanta. She mentioned a potential lead on a position opening in Charlotte. She wants to give me the details."

The grits turned to cement in his throat. He took a quick sip of the coffee, but it was hot, and went down the wrong way. He grabbed a napkin, covered his mouth and coughed. Vanessa's eyes widened and she lifted in her seat as if to run to his side. He held up a hand.

"I'm okay," he said between coughs. "It just went down the wrong way." He cleared his throat and took another, smaller sip. Once he composed himself, he gave Vanessa what he hoped was a that's-awesome smile. "When's the call?"

"Later this morning. She's doing the morning show right now. It might not mean anything."

"But it could mean everything. Would you want to move to Charlotte?"

She lifted a shoulder. "I'm not sure. I've visited the city, but I've never considered living there."

A dash of hope sprung in his chest. If she didn't want to move to Charlotte, then maybe she wouldn't. Maybe she'd find a job closer to Sunshine Beach. If that were the case, they'd have a better chance of keeping things going.

"But I'd go for the right opportunity," Vanessa said. "After realizing how many people doubted me, I owe it to myself to go after every opportunity. If this pans out, then I guess I'll be moving."

"That's great," Dion said with forced cheer.

The hesitancy in her expression melted away. She straightened her shoulders and met his gaze. "You really think so?"

"I do. Like you said, there's no need to let others' limitations hold you back. If you want it, go for it."

Her smile made him want to give her the world. "Thank you. I appreciate you supporting me."

Dion's smile felt like it was plastered onto his face. Stiff and unyielding. He didn't want her to leave, but the longer she stayed the faster she'd realize he and his small-town dreams weren't enough to make her happy.

"Everyone deserves to be encouraged to be great. I'd never try to hold you back."

Sheri came over with the coffeepot in her hand. "Want a refill?"

Dion held up his cup. "Please."

"I heard you interviewed for the division manager position yesterday," Sheri said as she poured the coffee.

He nodded, not surprised she'd found out. Everyone on his crew knew and was campaigning for Dion to get the job.

"Well, just in case that doesn't work out," Sheri said.

Vanessa hit her arm. "Don't say that."

Sheri shrugged. "I'm just saying. You never know what could happen. I hope it does, but if it doesn't you know my cousin is the planning director with the county."

Dion nodded. "Yeah."

"Well, he said their public works director is retiring. They're going to promote the deputy, which means they'll need a new deputy. I mentioned you."

He put down his coffee mug and sat up straight. "Why did you mention me?"

"Because you'd be great. I'm not saying the job is yours, I'm just saying if things don't work out at the town be on the lookout for the position with the county." Sheri smiled and walked away.

Vanessa tapped his hand. "Apply for it."

The position was bigger than the one he'd interviewed for. More responsibility, but it was a job he could do. A job, if he were honest, that he'd love to have. Except, he was already trying to advance where he was. "Nah."

"Why not?"

"Because I applied for the division manager position. I can't go applying for a job somewhere else."

"That makes no sense. Yes, you can."

"People in government talk. If I put in for that job, it'll make it look like I'm not happy at Sunshine Beach. Then they'll go with someone else."

Vanessa shook her head. "Or they'll realize other people are considering you and they don't need to let a good employee go. I say apply for it."

He shrugged. "I don't know. I've got seniority here and my crew like me."

"Then hire them when you're deputy director. Didn't you just encourage me to consider a lead in Charlotte? Take your own advice and consider this lead."

Dion shrugged and sipped his coffee. "Let me see what happens with the position first."

Chapter Twenty-Three

Vanessa watched as Dion meticulously walked back and forth in straight lines to spread a winter fertilizer with a manual spreader across his backyard. She sat in a plastic chair on his patio and sipped from a glass filled with sweet tea. For the past few weeks as they waited for Tyrone's contact to give a date for her grandmother's investigation, they'd fallen into a routine. She continued to look for jobs and follow up on leads during the day while Dion worked. In the afternoons, she came by and watched him do odd jobs around his home or he came to her place and talked to her about what she'd researched during the day. He'd taken her on another ghost investigation, and even though she wasn't a believer, she was still fascinated by what they learned as they researched the property.

"It looks like we're getting closer to the investigation at my grandmother's place," she said when he was close to the patio.

"That's what Tyrone told me," Dion said as he spread fertilizer parallel to the edge of the patio.

"I still can't believe how fast he set this up."

Dion finished his work and put the spreader on the patio. "Tyrone moves quickly. Not only does he work at the radio station, but he works the promotional parties thrown by the media company that owns the station. When he's not investigating on weekends he'll go to Atlanta, Charlotte and LA occasionally for parties. He's run into a few celebrities because of that."

"Why hasn't he moved away if he's so interested in getting involved in show business?" Of the three brothers, Tyrone gave off the most "bright lights, big city" ambitions.

Dion rolled up the half-empty bag of fertilizer he'd left on the patio. "Tyrone wants the glitz and glamour but he's also a small-town guy. He likes to go out there and have fun, meet people, but since our parents are gone, I don't think he wants to be too far away from me and Wes."

"Are you telling me he's sentimental?"

"Kinda," Dion said. "Though he'll never admit it. The same with Wes. He's worked for an architectural firm for about six or seven years but has gotten offers from other places. He always turns them down and decides to stay close."

She sipped her tea. "What would happen if one of you did move away?"

Dion's brows furled and he picked up the extra glass of tea on the table next to her. "I don't know. I mean, we'd be fine, but it would be weird to not have my brothers around."

They were silent for a few minutes before she broached her next subject. "Have you heard anything about the position yet?"

Dion's slight hesitation before he put down the glass was the only hint of his reaction. He hadn't mentioned anything about the interview except to say his boss was still interviewing and deciding. Though he tried to pretend as if it weren't bothering him, Vanessa could see the tension in his shoulders and the way he changed the subject whenever she brought it up.

"The end of last week, Joe mentioned they were getting close but hadn't made a choice yet."

"He told you that?" It was the first direct update he'd told her about.

"No, one of my guys asked his administrative assistant and told me. I don't even know if that's the truth or not."

"It's been four weeks. That's a long time to drag things out."

"This is local government," he said, as if that made it better. "They drag everything out."

"Did you apply for the deputy position Sheri mentioned?"

He turned away and picked up the spreader and bag of fertilizer. "Not yet. It didn't post until a few days ago."

"Don't wait too late or else you'll talk yourself out of it."

"I haven't talked myself into it so how can I talk myself out of it?" He walked toward the shed.

Vanessa jumped up and followed him. "Why are you hesitating? You're qualified for the job."

"Qualifications don't mean a thing. Why would I rock the boat where I'm at for a job at a place I know nothing about?"

"Because they're dragging their feet giving you a promotion you deserve. I don't think they appreciate you and you're underestimating yourself. When I'm gone I'd hate to think of you still sitting in that job being taken advantage of."

He tossed the bag into a corner of the shed. "When you're gone? You say that as if you're leaving soon."

"Well… I may be."

He spun and faced her. "What?"

"The station manager my friend mentioned called me back. They want me to come up next week for an interview. If things work out, then…"

"You'll really move that far away?"

The disbelief in his tone tapped on guilt she didn't want to feel.

"Yes, Dion, the plan was always for me to move

once I found a job." Her words held more bite than she'd wanted. A defensive reaction to the hurt in his voice. She hadn't come here to settle down and change for some guy. She'd come here to get herself together before taking the next step in her life. She wouldn't feel bad about walking away from Dion for this opportunity. No matter how much the idea of leaving him made her heart ache.

He watched her for several beats before turning and putting the spreader in the back corner. "What day is the interview?"

"Thursday."

"Good. You'll do good. You'll get it." He didn't look her way as he walked out.

Vanessa hurried behind him. "It's not guaranteed."

"What was the phone call like when you touched base with them?"

"It was good. They'd seen my work. They said my personality was what they were looking for."

"See, shoo-in." He stomped over to the patio and picked up both glasses from the table.

"I'm going for my dreams and what I want. I want the same thing for you, too."

"I'm going after what I want."

"But…"

He spun around. "But what? I shouldn't be happy with the life I've got? I shouldn't be okay with living in a small beach town, working with my crew and taking care of the people I grew up with who took care of me when I needed them? Is everyone supposed to chase big dreams and dollar signs?"

"That's not what I'm saying."

"Good, because if that's the type of guy you want, then you came to the wrong place. I'm not him and I never will be."

"I'm not trying to change you. I'm just encouraging you—"

"I've been *encouraged* before. I don't need it. I'm good with where I'm at and what I'm doing. Save that encouragement for your next guy." He turned away from her and went to his back door.

Save it for her next guy. The words were an unexpected punch to the gut. She'd known this was short term. She'd insisted they remember that. Still, the finality in his words, the lack of emotion as he talked about her with another guy, reminded her that just because Dion was sweet and had taken care of her didn't mean he cared for her. They'd agreed to hook up. Exclusively hook up, but that was it.

What had she expected anyway? That she'd go to Charlotte and continue a relationship with him when she was away?

Yes, that's exactly what you'd begun to think.

She shook her head. "You know what. I think I'm going to head back to my place."

"Cool," Dion said without flinching.

Vanessa waited for more. When he didn't say anything, she rolled her eyes, turned and walked away.

Chapter Twenty-Four

Dion sat at his dining room table. The house was dark except for the glow from his laptop screen. He stared at the flashing cursor in the "Name" section of the online application. He'd stared at the online application for thirty minutes and still hadn't filled out the damn form.

He leaned back in the chair and covered his face with his hands. He let out a long sigh followed by a loud groan. Damn, Vanessa, his brothers, Sheri and their encouragement.

He knew they meant well, but their pushes made him feel as if he wasn't good enough. He wasn't ambitious enough. He was the old boring guy his ex accused him of being. The guy he'd become at nineteen when his parents died.

He'd done what he had to do back then and wouldn't change a single decision he'd made. Giving up a scholarship to attend college out of state, taking the job as a laborer just because he needed stability and benefits for his brothers. He'd let go of dreams for himself in favor of keeping what remained of his family together. The aunts and uncles from out of town who'd tried to swoop in and take care of him, Wes and Tyrone all said he wouldn't be able to handle the responsibility. That he was a child himself and they were better off leaving and coming with them. Dion had known different. They'd lost their parents, they didn't need to lose their home, friends and the remaining stability they had.

He'd proved them all wrong, and he'd watched Wes study harder and get a full ride to Clemson University. He'd pushed Tyrone enough to make him focus and channel his love of music and partying into a career at the radio station and promoting. His brothers were happy and successful, and he'd been a part of that.

No, he'd never take back what he'd done, but that didn't make it easy to stop thinking about what others needed versus what he wanted. To get off autopilot survival mode and get back into a mindset he hadn't had since he was nineteen years old.

He pushed back from the table and jumped up

from the chair. Frustration crawled across his skin like a million ants. Yes, he wanted to do more. Yes, he wanted more control. Yes, he wanted for the higher-ups to listen to his ideas and suggestions and not appear surprised that Dion could make a smart decision.

He wanted the promotion because he could do the job. He could do that job and a lot more. Who were they to say just because he didn't pin his future on becoming a reality TV star meant he was somehow settling for less?

Before he knew it, he'd snatched up the keys to his truck and was behind the wheel. He didn't know who he was going to set straight first. His brothers or Vanessa. His subconscious made the decision and Dion drove to Vanessa's place.

The lights glowed behind the curtains. It was nine thirty in the evening. Just around the time Vanessa went to bed. Early like him.

He was on the porch and ringing the doorbell right as the first whispers of doubt tickled his brain. He was showing up, unannounced, after they hadn't necessarily gotten into an argument but had parted with hard feelings brewing. She might tell him to get the hell off her porch and never call her again. She'd have every right to do so.

Vanessa opened the door before he could let that thought kill his bravado. She'd changed into her lounging clothes. A pair of leggings, a black tank top and a long pink cardigan sweater she favored.

Her hair was wrapped in a black satin cap, her skin free of all makeup. She looked like she was ready to crawl into bed. The urge to crawl in next to her made him step closer.

"What are you doing here?" she asked in a tight voice.

Her frosty tone stopped him from reaching for her. He got back to the reason why he'd driven over here in the first place. "We need to talk."

"About what? Did you come over here just to tell me again about all the ways I'm trying to change you or you're not good enough?"

"Will you just let me in?"

She glared and he expected to hear the "get off my porch" he'd imagined when he rang the bell. Instead she huffed, rolled her eyes, then turned away and went into the house. She left the door open. Dion took that as an invitation and followed her into the living room.

She crossed her arms and glared at him. "Talk."

"Look, I'm happy with my life," he said.

"No one said you weren't," she shot back.

"I'm tired of people telling me I don't want more than what I have."

She looked skyward as if searching for patience before speaking again. "No one is saying you don't want more."

"I like what I do, and I want to keep doing it. Do I want to make things better? Yes. Am I capable of doing more than what I'm doing now? Maybe. But—"

"But what, Dion? The answer isn't *maybe*. The answer is *yes*. You took care of your brothers, got a job and even went back for your degree online without a complaint. Of course you can do whatever you set your mind to. If you don't want me to encourage you, then I won't. Like you said, I'll be gone soon and what I think doesn't matter."

She turned away from him. Dion hurried forward and touched her elbow. The look she gave him made him drop his hand.

"What you think does matter. It matters a hell of a lot more than I want it to. Do you think I don't want to be the kind of guy you deserve? The kind of guy who can give you the life you want?"

She rushed forward and poked a finger in his chest. "I never asked you to change for me. I don't want you to change. I love you for the person you are, not for someone I imagine you to be."

"But how long will that last?" He froze, then shook his head. "Hold up. Did you say—"

"Stop!" She held up her hands. "Just…stop." She took a deep breath and spun away from him. "I didn't mean it like that."

Dion came up behind her. He wanted to grab her shoulders, spin her around. Did she love him? "Then why can't you look at me?"

"Because I'm embarrassed," she said over her shoulder. When she spoke again, her voice was softer. "Look, Dion, I didn't mean to imply that you and what you do aren't enough. You are, but you're also so much more. You're sincere, down-to-earth and you have a good heart. I don't want you to forget that or let other people take advantage of you. You deserve the promotion at work, but you're capable of the job Sheri mentioned, and you're capable of being on a television show dedicated to doing something you love. I believe in you and I want you to believe in yourself."

"I'm scared," he blurted out.

Vanessa spun around. "What could you possibly be afraid of?"

He cringed and ran a hand over his face. He hadn't meant to drop out all of his secrets, his worst fears. When he looked at Vanessa again, he expected to see pity or mocking but only compassion filled her brown eyes.

"I'm afraid of trying and being laughed at. Or worse, going for it, getting it and being out of my element. Everything I've done I did because I had no other choice. I took care of Wes and Tyrone while they finished high school because it was the right choice. I took the job with the town and put up with the supervisors who believed I wouldn't understand anything that required me to use my brain and their low expectations to keep food on the table and provide health insurance for my brothers."

Vanessa reached up and took his face in her hands. "What you did for your brothers is amazing. You put your dreams aside for them and I understand that. You didn't have options then, but you do now. Look

at what you've accomplished. Dion, you're amazing.
You're capable. You're strong."

Dion's hands shook as he clutched Vanessa's
waist. He'd heard those words from his brothers, his
employees, his friends. Heard them over and over
but never allowed himself to believe them. Despite
resenting the expectations to fail, he'd also absorbed
those labels. Just a laborer. Not cut out for manage-
ment. Good where you are. Boring and going nowhere. He'd accepted them and let them hold him
back. He didn't want to be held back anymore.

"What if I can't?" he asked.

"Then I'll help you regroup and figure out the
next steps."

"Why?"

"Why not?"

Because she would leave. Because a relationship
between them may not last. Because he didn't deserve to hold her back from her own dreams. All reasons he'd like to give, but when she looked at him
with those eyes, none of those reasons mattered. The
emotions bubbling up in his chest were too big and
too vast to explore. His body buzzed with the need to
laugh, cry, run and whoop with joy. They all mingled
and coalesced into one urgent need to have Vanessa
in his arms, his life.

He lowered his mouth and kissed her. The kiss
was fueled by the overwhelming disbelief that a
woman as beautiful, brilliant and talented as Vanessa
could somehow fall in love with him. Her soft sigh

before her arms wrapped around his neck made his heart jackhammer. Dion pushed the cardigan off her shoulders onto the floor. In a breath, the kiss became frantic, their hands tugging and jerking until their shirts hit the floor and Vanessa's breasts were free.

He pulled her close. The tips of her nipples against his chest were better than any treat he'd ever indulged in. Her hands unbuttoned his pants and pushed them off his hips. Her soft fingers wrapped around him and he sucked in a breath. His hand palmed the back of her head. The satin of her cap blocked access to her hair. He jerked it off her head and dug his fingers into her thick tresses as she slowly massaged him almost to completion.

He quickly led her to the bedroom. They fell onto the bed in a tangle of arms and legs. Vanessa pulled a condom out of the side drawer and slowly covered his length. Her eyes met his as she lowered onto him. Surrounding him in the tight, slick heat of her. Their eyes met as she moved. First slowly and then gradually faster and faster. Desire mingled with something else in the depths of her brown eyes. Something deeper that tapped into a powerful need only she could fulfill. How in the world was he ever going to let her go?

Chapter Twenty-Five

Vanessa returned to Sunshine Beach after her interview with the Charlotte station with a smile on her face and a skip in her step. Everything had gone better than she could have even imagined. They wanted her as their new morning show anchor, but they also wanted her to cohost a Sunday talk show highlighting stories in the community. Not only did they love her energy, but no one balked when she mentioned her ultimate goal was to investigate and present hard-hitting stories as well.

Vanessa had to pinch herself constantly during the ride back to be sure she wasn't dreaming. She'd hoped to find something even better than her last job, but she hadn't expected to find something so great. Everything in her life was falling into place and she couldn't be happier. Including her relationship with Dion.

She didn't want to believe taking a job in a city hundreds of miles away would be the end of them. She'd spent her free time reading about all the ways to make long-distance relationships work. There was weekend travel, video chats and app-controlled sex toys to keep their connection strong when they were apart. So many other people had made long-distance relationships work. Why couldn't she and Dion do the same?

Because he hasn't agreed to keeping this going once you move away.

She pushed that pessimistic thought away. There was no way he could make love to her the way he had, or encourage her like he had, if he didn't care. Even when she'd tossed out the "love you" phrase, he hadn't panicked and run. That had to count for something.

Dion had to work, so they'd agreed to meet up later for dinner after he was off, and she had time to settle after her quick trip. Her grandmother called just as she'd gotten out of the shower.

"I just want to give you a heads-up," was the first thing Arletha greeted her with in an ominous tone.

"Heads-up about what?" Vanessa adjusted the towel she'd wrapped around her body.

"I heard it through the grapevine that Dion didn't get the job."

Vanessa gripped the phone and sank heavily on the bed. She trembled, partly from the chill in the room on her damp body and partially with suppressed anger. She'd worried that would be the outcome when they took so long to decide, yet she'd held out hope that maybe she was wrong. "Why not?"

"Because his boss hired his cousin Chad in from solid waste. It wasn't easy. Even the people downtown wondered about the choice. That's why it took so long to make the final decision. They had to jump through hoops to justify his decision and prevent a potential lawsuit."

"They think Dion's going to sue them?"

"I don't know, but they dug up every reason they could think of for why they hired that guy rather than Dion. They told him at the end of his shift today."

Vanessa grunted and scowled. "That's horrible. Dion deserves better. I'm glad he applied for the job at the county."

Her grandmother sighed. "That's the other thing. I found out today that the county did a quick round of interviews because they already had someone else in mind. They've filled their position, too. That won't work out for him."

"What? Already?"

"Already. I really feel bad for Dion. He's such a good worker and can do so much more, but the people around here want to keep him where they feel comfortable. Have you talked to him?"

"Not yet. We're going to dinner later."

"Well, send him my love when you do. I know this must be rough, but he'll get through. He always does."

"I know." She just hoped he didn't take this setback as proof he shouldn't wish for more. He'd been so open, so vulnerable, when he'd confessed his feelings about being afraid to reach for more. He'd just become comfortable with stepping out of his comfort zone. This type of blow could push him back into the shell he'd used to protect himself.

She wanted to call him and ask what happened, but also didn't want to make him self-conscious knowing the word had gotten around and everyone knew how he'd been screwed out of the position he deserved. She opted to text him and let him know she was back in town and looking forward to dinner.

I'll see you in thirty minutes. Dress up. was his return text.

Thirty minutes later, Dion rang her doorbell. The smile on his face when she opened the door didn't give any hint of him having a bad day. He was dressed in dark slacks and a cream-colored button-up shirt and he held out a bouquet of red roses to her.

"Welcome back," he said in a rumbling voice she wanted to listen to for the rest of her life.

Vanessa took the flowers in one hand and slid forward to hug him. His strong arms encircled her waist and pulled her in close. The solid comfort of his body and the warmth of him seeped into her soul and told her she was home. She breathed deep of him and finally relaxed after three days of whirl-wind travel and business.

"I'm happy to be back," she said.

He smiled down at her. "I hope you're happy and hungry. I made reservations at the steakhouse across town and then after that we're having dessert at the cake shop downtown."

"Roses at the door and I don't have to think about where to go and eat. You're trying to spoil me, and I like it."

Dion chuckled. "Good. Put the roses down and we can get going."

A few minutes later, they were in Dion's truck driving to the restaurant. He reached over and threaded his fingers with hers.

"How did it go? They love you, don't they?" His voice was eager and encouraging.

Vanessa studied him for any sign of hesitation or discouragement. Dion glanced at her and raised his brows. Nothing but support and interest in his gaze.

"They like me," she said. "They want me to be one of their morning anchors and also cohost a weekend show on the community."

Dion squeezed and shook her hand. "What did I tell you! I knew you'd find something better than the job you had. Didn't I tell you that you're great?"

Vanessa laughed, caught up by his obvious enthusiasm for her good news. "You did."

"When do they want you to start?"

Her smile dimmed. "In four weeks."

He glanced at her and the edges of his smile softened. "Then we've got four weeks to get you ready to move."

"Dion... I..."

He squeezed her hand. "Hey, it's okay. We'll figure this out."

Her heart mimicked a hummingbird. She turned to him with wide eyes. "You want to figure this out?"

He nodded slowly, then gave her a what-have-I-got-to-lose half smile. "I do. What about you?"

She let out a breath and squeezed his hand. "I do. It'll be hard."

"A lot of things are hard. That doesn't mean you don't try to do them anyway."

She tilted her head to the side. "Look at you. Walking on the wild side."

Dion chuckled. "I wouldn't say all that. I'm just listening to what you and my brothers kept saying. If I want something, go for it." He glanced at her. "I want you, Vanessa."

Her heart squeezed and she bit the corner of her lip. "I want you, too."

They were quiet for several moments. The night was starting so well she wanted to keep things light, but she couldn't hold back. "My grandmother told me you're not getting the job."

Dion's fingers twitched in her hand. She held on tighter so he wouldn't pull back.

"I'm good," he said in a voice that was too calm to be real.

"Still, I didn't want you to feel bad because of…" He glanced up when her voice trailed off.

"I don't feel bad about your good news. I'm happy for you. You deserve that position and more. This setback at work is only that. A setback. Right now, let's focus on your grandmother's investigation and getting you ready for the move to Charlotte."

"But—"

"No *buts*, Vanessa. I'm serious. I'll be okay. Don't let that place ruin this night. Not when I missed you when you were gone. We'll worry about my job, our relationship, everything another day. I've gotten through worse. We'll get through this."

Chapter Twenty-Six

Vanessa sat next to her grandmother on the couch while Dion and his brothers went over their plans for the investigation with the producer for the Exploration Channel. Arletha watched with excitement and anticipation. Vanessa could barely sit still. She shifted and readjusted her position on the couch every few seconds. She wasn't sure what, if anything, Dion and his brothers would discover but she was anxious about giving her grandmother answers and closure.

Arletha rubbed her hands back and forth on her thighs. She'd dressed nicely but casually for the filming in a pair of black slacks and a red button-up shirt, her hair freshly pressed and curled from a visit to the salon earlier in the day, and her makeup flawless.

"I don't know why I'm so nervous," her grand-mother said. "I know it's him."

Vanessa reached over and placed her hand over her grandmother's. "It's the camera. That's all."

"I just want to know what he has to tell me."

Vanessa squeezed her grandmother's hand. "Don't worry. The brothers want to help you get answers."

"I know they do." A smile broke out over her grandmother's face. "I wonder if I'll see him. Like in the movie *Ghost*."

Vanessa shook her head and chuckled. "I don't think it works like that."

Arletha lifted a shoulder. "Still. It would be pretty cool."

"As much as I miss Granddad, I think I'd rather not actually see his spirit. That might be too much for me."

Her grandmother laughed and patted Vanessa's hand. She leaned over and whispered, "It might be too much for me, too."

Vanessa was glad to see her grandmother's shoulders relax and the nervous bounce in her leg stop. Even though she didn't believe in ghosts, today she wished they existed for her grandmother's sake. If they went through all of this and found nothing, that would break her grandmother's heart.

Dion and the rest finished going over the equipment and the setup and walked over to Vanessa and her grandmother. Dion gave her a reassuring smile and sat on the arm of the couch next to Vanessa.

"Alright, we're ready to get started," Tyrone said. "Dorian is going to record everything." Tyrone pointed to the man holding the camera.

"Just pretend I'm not here," Dorian said. He was short and thick with a pleasant face and big welcoming smile.

Her grandmother nodded. "I'll try."

Tyrone pointed to the woman next to him. "Tiana is here to observe what we do firsthand and make sure we're all in good positions for the camera."

Tiana was average height, curvy with dark brown skin and thick curly hair pulled back into a huge poof at the back of her head. Her dark eyes were bright with anticipation as her gaze went from Tyrone back to Vanessa and her grandmother.

"I've been excited about the idea for this show ever since Tyrone first told me about what him and his brothers do. I also know this is a very personal and important day for you, Mrs. Montgomery. I respect that and hope we can give you the answers you're looking for."

Her grandmother nodded. "Thank you very much. Can we get started now?"

They all laughed. Tyrone nodded. "Yes, let's get started."

Tiana nodded. "Sounds great to me."

After they interviewed her grandmother about her life in the house with her grandfather and the reason she believed his spirit was still there, they recorded a few snippets of the brothers discussing what they do and how they planned to investigate. Dion, Tyrone and Wesley's good-natured relationship shone through as they talked about why they enjoy helping people.

The entire time Vanessa stayed in the background and tried not to interfere. Just like last time, she was impressed by how professional they were when they worked. Though they were relaxed with her grandmother, there was a subtle shift to a more serious and professional tone when they explained their process.

When they finally made it upstairs to her grandmother's bedroom, Vanessa was just as anxious as her grandmother to start the investigation.

"Alright, Mrs. Montgomery," Dion said once Tiana had everyone in the best spot for the camera. "We're going to start with the EMF to check for any unusual energy."

Vanessa held her breath as Dion turned on the EMF and slowly walked through the room. Her eyes focused on the red button at the top as she waited for the light to come on or flicker as it had done during the other investigations. After several long seconds, nothing happened.

Wesley held up his phone with the voice app. "Let's see if he's willing to talk to us." Wesley turned on the device and the sounds of static radio filled the room. "Hey, Mr. Montgomery, are you here?"

The tension in the room increased as the static crackled and everyone waited. There was no response.

Wesley licked his lips and tried again. "It's okay.

We're all friends here. We just want to find out what's going on with you."

More tense moments passed as everyone focused on the device in his hand. Her grandmother slid closer to Wesley with a hand pressed to her chest.

"Tyrone, are you seeing anything?" Dion asked.

Tyrone held a night vision camera. Tyrone panned the camera around the darkening room. He looked up and shook his head. "Nah, nothing."

"Let's try other areas of the house. Where else have you felt his presence, Mrs. Montgomery?" Dion asked.

Arletha pointed toward the bathroom. "Sometimes in there and also in the sitting room."

"Alright, we'll check all of that."

Forty minutes later and they still had nothing. Vanessa watched as her grandmother's excitement waned to disappointment. Each room was quiet and still.

"Let's call it a night," Wesley said after they'd checked everywhere and were back in the living room.

"Are we giving up?" Arletha asked.

Dion shook his head. "No way, Mrs. Montgomery. Sometimes the spirits don't want to talk when we want them to. We'll go with our plan to spend the night. We'll keep the night vision camera going in our room and the EMF on. If there's nothing tonight, we'll try again tomorrow." He looked over at Tiana. "Is that okay with you?"

Tiana nodded. "That's fine with me. Tomorrow

morning we'll get up and get some shots of the town, along with you and your brothers giving us some background on the haunted history in the area. Tyrone says you usually spend a day researching. We can get some footage of you doing that and the background of Mrs. Montgomery's home."

"Great. Let's all relax and get some rest," Dion said.

Her grandmother gave a stiff nod. "I'll...show everyone where you can sleep tonight."

Vanessa placed a hand on her grandmother's shoulder. "Are you okay?"

Arletha shook off Vanessa's hand. "I'm fine, child. I'm just fine." She smiled at Tiana and Dorian. "Follow me and I'll show you which guest bedrooms to use."

Vanessa didn't say anything and let her grandmother get everyone settled. Dion walked over and rubbed her lower back. "I'm sorry."

"It's not your fault."

"Still, I know your grandmother was really hoping to get answers tonight."

Tyrone walked over. "It's the first night. Sometimes that happens. That doesn't mean we're giving up."

Wes joined them and nodded firmly. "Not at all. Even if Tiana and Dorian have to leave on Monday, we'll still help Mrs. Montgomery."

All three agreed. Vanessa's heart warmed. "I appreciate you guys looking out for my grandmother. I was nervous about leaving next week for Charlotte but knowing she has you all makes it easier."

Dion's hand froze on her back for a second before it fell away. "We won't let her down." He looked at his brothers. "Let's get our stuff out of the car."

Vanessa watched them walk away with a heavy heart. She tried not to bring up her leaving, but it wasn't something they could avoid. The station had helped her find a place to live and she was scheduled to start in two weeks. She and Dion hadn't changed their minds about not breaking up after she left, but a part of her worried. Could they really keep things going once she was hundreds of miles away?

Later that night, Vanessa knocked on her grandmother's door. It was just past ten and the house was quiet as everyone settled in their rooms. Vanessa couldn't sleep. She was worried about her grandmother after a disappointing first night.

After tossing and turning, she'd opted to get up and grab a drink of water before trying to sleep again. When she noticed the light on under her grandmother's door, she'd decided to check in.

Arletha opened the door with a worried expression. "Vanessa, is everything okay?"

Vanessa nodded. "It is. I saw your light on. I decided to check on you."

Her grandmother's concerned frown switched to an appreciative smile. "I'm fine. A little disappointed, but I'm okay."

"We'll figure out what's going on. Dion and his

brothers said they'll continue to investigate even after I'm in Charlotte."

"I know they will. Your granddad was always stubborn. I should have known he wouldn't show up when I want him to."

"Try and get some sleep. We've all got a lot to do tomorrow."

Arletha nodded. "I will. Now go to bed and stop worrying about me."

Vanessa leaned in and kissed her grandmother's cheek. "Fine. Good night."

"Good night."

Vanessa stared at her grandmother's closed bedroom door for a few seconds. The light went off on the other side and she sighed. If they didn't find anything this weekend, she'd make an effort to visit Sunshine Beach as soon as she could. She'd also ask her mom and sister to try to visit. She took comfort knowing Dion would keep her updated.

She went downstairs and flipped on the light in the kitchen. Instead of opting for cold water in the fridge, she went to the pantry and pulled out one of the bottles of water her grandmother kept there. She opened the top and was heading back to her room when Dion walked into the kitchen. He'd changed out of the jeans and T-shirt he'd worn earlier into a pair of dark gray sweatpants and a long-sleeved navy shirt that clung to his chest and shoulders like a second skin.

His eyes widened before his lips lifted. "What are you doing down here?"

She lifted the bottle in her hand. "Thirsty. What about you?"

He walked over and stood close enough for her to smell the fresh scent of the soap he used in the shower. "Same. That and I couldn't sleep."

"Really? I thought you'd be out by now."

He placed a hand on her hip and pulled her closer. "I usually am, but I don't have your warm body beside me. Instead, I've got Tyrone snoring on the top bunk, and Wesley mumbling in his sleep in the other bed."

Vanessa chuckled and wrapped an arm around his neck. Instead of taking separate bedrooms, the brothers opted to share one of the rooms her grandmother used for kids when the place was a bed-and-breakfast.

"You could always sneak into the room and sleep with me."

His brows drew together. "I'm a grown-ass man. I don't have to sneak."

Vanessa's brows rose. "Oh, well, then why haven't you joined me?"

"I knocked. You didn't answer. That's why I'm down here." He grinned and lowered his head.

She breathed into his kiss and held him tighter. "I'm going to miss you so much."

He rested his forehead on hers. "I already miss you."

"We're going to be okay, right?"

He nodded and lifted his head. "More than okay."

His voice was confident and strong, but his eyes were worried.

"Then we won't think about how much we're going to miss each other. Instead, we're going to enjoy the time we have together," she said.

"I like that idea."

He took her hand in his and led her back to the stairs. They were just at the top of the stairs when the door to the room the brothers shared burst open. Tyrone and Wesley rushed out.

"Dion, where you been?" Wesley asked.

Dion frowned at his brothers. "What's wrong?"

Tyron pointed to the EMF in Wesley's hand. "It was going off like crazy, bruh. Something is definitely going on."

Vanessa's heart jumped. "What? When?" She stared at the dark instrument.

"It just stopped." Tyrone held up the night vision camera. "We were going to check and see if we can catch anything."

A loud crash shook the hall followed by her grandmother's shriek. Vanessa gasped and her stomach dropped. She turned and ran down the hall. The light in her grandmother's room turned on. She pushed open the door without knocking.

"Grandma! What happened?"

Arletha sat on the side of the bed with her arms crossed. She didn't appear hurt, just annoyed. "Your granddad."

"What? I heard a crash and you screamed."

"That's because he scared me. He knocked the picture off the wall." Arletha pointed across the room.

Sure enough, the picture on the wall that usually hung next to the chest of drawers lay shattered in pieces on the floor. Dion and his brothers hurried into the room after her. Wesley walked over to the broken frame. The EMF immediately started buzzing.

Vanessa sucked in a breath at the same time her grandmother gasped. Arletha jumped up from the bed and hurried toward Wesley. Vanessa grabbed her arm to stop her.

"The glass." Vanessa pointed to the floor.

Dion and Tyrone joined Wesley. Tyrone held up the night vision camera. Dion pulled his cell phone out of his sweatpants pocket and opened the spirit box app. Footsteps sounded in the hall a second before Tiana and Dorian rushed inside. Dorian already had the camera on his shoulder.

"We heard the commotion and figured something had happened," Tiana said.

"The picture fell off the wall," Vanessa said. The EMF continued to buzz. "And there's that."

"Is it him?" her grandmother asked.

Dion glanced at Arletha and gave her a hopeful smile. "Let's find out." He took a deep breath and held up his phone. "Hey, Mr. Montgomery, is that you?"

Everyone stilled as the static crackled for several agonizing breaths. "It's okay, Mr. Montgomery. We just wanna holla at you for a second."

The sound of static filled the room before it dipped away and what sounded an awful like the word "Yes" came through Dion's phone.

Arletha gasped and pressed a hand to her mouth. Vanessa wrapped her arms around her grandmother's shoulder.

Dion looked back at them and nodded slowly. "Okay. You know you scared Mrs. Montgomery, right? Did you need to talk to her?"

More static before a garbled sound similar to "Help" came through. Her grandmother shivered. Vanessa frowned as she looked at the worried expressions on the brothers' faces.

"You need help?" Dion asked.

Vanessa's heart was stuck in her throat as she waited for some response. This time when the sound of "Yes" came through, she shivered just as much as her grandmother.

"Is that why you knocked down the picture? Tell us what you need. We'll try and help you."

Tiana slid closer to Dion and his brothers and she waved Dorian to follow. Vanessa still clung to her grandmother as she watched. The static buzzed and echoed in the silent room as they all waited. "Ring."

Dion frowned. He exchanged a look with his brothers before turning to Vanessa. "Ring? What ring?" he repeated.

Arletha's shoulders slumped. "My wedding ring. I lost it right before he died." Tears came to her grandmother's eyes. "He asked me about it right before his heart attack. He can't rest because I lost it." Her voice broke.

Vanessa hugged her grandmother closer. She felt powerless. "No, Grandma, don't think like that."

The EMF buzzed erratically. The static in the voice box grew louder before a very clear "Floor" came through.

Vanessa stared at Dion. "I heard that. What does it mean?"

Wesley snapped and his eyes widened. "The floor. Check the floor." He put the EMF on the top of the chest of drawers and lowered to his knees. Dion and Tyrone followed suit.

"The glass. Be careful," Vanessa called out.

The brothers nodded, but quickly went about moving the broken frame and the larger pieces of glass. They checked the area where the picture had fallen, but there was nothing on the floor. Dion bent over to grab another larger piece of glass and froze. His head lifted and he stared up at Vanessa and then her grandmother with wide eyes.

"I think I figured it out." He jumped up. "Help me move this." He went to one end of the chest of drawers. His brothers hurried to the other. They slowly pushed it away from the wall. Dion lowered on his haunches and reached into the space they'd cleared. When he stood up, he held a ring in his hand.

Arletha gasped. She rushed over to him, no thoughts or cares about the glass on the floor. "My ring!"

Dion handed the gold band with a sparkling diamond cluster out to her. Arletha took the ring with so much care. She pressed it to her chest, then lifted it to her lips and kissed it. "I thought I lost it." She inspected it and then gasped.

Vanessa rushed over. "What is it?"

Her grandmother pressed trembling fingers to her lips. "It's engraved. *To my only love.*" Tears streamed down her face. "He got it engraved."

"You didn't lose it, Grandma. It must have gotten lost after Granddad got that done."

Arletha's shoulders shook as she cried. "He fell right here in this room. Right in this spot. That's where I found him. When he later..." She swallowed hard. "I didn't think to look under there."

"You wouldn't have," Vanessa said. "But you found it."

Dion stepped forward. "He wanted you to find it."

Arletha grinned and wiped her eyes. "Dammit, Lou, is that why you stuck around? Just so I could find this?"

The static from the voice box lowered. "Love. You." The lights flickered and the EMF stopped buzzing.

Vanessa's eyes widened as she searched the room. The hum of electricity she'd felt but hadn't noticed a second before disappeared. She turned to Dion, who gave her a small smile.

Arletha glanced around the room. Tears trailed down her face again and she slipped the ring on her finger. "I love you, too."

Chapter Twenty-Seven

Dion's work cell phone rang just as he pulled his truck into its designated parking space at the end of another long day. Winter was typically a slower time for them. Fewer storms, less grass growing, fewer calls. This winter had decided to be completely different thanks to the fickleness of South Carolina weather. They'd had a winter thunderstorm that took down trees and power lines, only for temperatures to dip toward freezing levels, which burst water lines, iced over roads and made the potholes grow like weeds.

The ridiculous winter weather not only made work exceedingly busy but also made it nearly impossible for him to get to Charlotte to see Vanessa. With Valentine's Day approaching, he really hoped he'd be able to get away and see her. The forecast for that weekend was cold, freezing rain, and he hoped and prayed the forecast was wrong.

He pulled his cell phone out of his back pocket and checked the number. He answered the call while the rest of the crew got out of the truck. "What's up, Tyrone?"

"We got it!" His brother's excited cry made Dion pull the phone away from his ear.

"Got what?" Dion asked.

Tyrone sucked his teeth, then continued in a quieter tone. "Man, the show. Tiana called me. They want to do the show. They've agreed to ten episodes. They want to start filming this spring. We've got to go to Atlanta to discuss all the details."

Dion slowly got out of the truck. His head spun with his brother's words. He placed a hand on the hood and looked around for signs of a hidden camera or other potential pranksters. All he saw were the other crews arriving and going back into the building.

"Wait, are you serious? They really want to make our show?"

"Why do you sound so surprised, Dion? I told you our show would be picked up. I told you we could do it."

"You did. I just…" Dion ran a hand over his face and laughed. "Are you playing with me?"

"I'm not playing. I'm all the way for real. We've

got a show. If it does well, then we'll get more episodes next season."

Dion covered his mouth with this hand, but he couldn't suppress the smile. Disbelief mingled with joy as Tyrone's words sunk in. They were really going to get picked up. A network really thought he and his brothers had what it took to have a television show. They believed in them, what they did, and thought it was worth something. He'd been so afraid to believe it could happen. So afraid to dream of something else, that he'd been avoiding asking Tyrone if he'd heard anything from Tiana and focused on other dreams to pursue.

"Tyrone, this is all because of you, man."

"Nah, it's because of us. We did this together."

"No, you were the one with the connection. You sold the idea of what we could do and believed in this from the start. We wouldn't be here without you, and I want you to know I recognize that. Good job, brother."

"Yeah, well, save all that for once we sign the contract. I can't believe it, but I do at the same time. Look, I've got to call Wesley and tell him. Drinks at my house later. Then we can plan to go to Atlanta to meet with the execs and talk about the show."

"Sounds like a plan. I'm going to try to get out of here as soon as I can."

"Do that. Just think, you may be able to quit that job one day."

Dion chuckled. He'd be able to sooner than expected. "Already working on that."

"Oh for real?" Tyrone sounded surprised.

"I'll tell you about that later. I didn't want to jinx it, but hopefully we'll have two things to celebrate soon."

"I can't wait to hear. See you later."

Dion hung up the phone and grinned. Their show was picked up. He pumped his fist as he walked into the building.

Once inside, Bobby, his crew chief, met him at the door with a sour expression. "Dion, Chad is waiting for you in the office. He doesn't look happy."

Dion closed his eyes and took a deep breath. He'd assumed working for Chad wasn't going to be easy, but he hadn't counted on the man nitpicking everything Dion did. It didn't help that most of the time the people in the division still came to Dion for direction. He was probably there to lecture Dion about not undermining him anymore.

Dion's cell phone chimed. He glanced down. He had a new email. He quickly touched the email application. The very first email at the top made Dion's breath catch. He opened it with nervous fingers.

"Mr. Jackson, we'd like to offer you the position of public works director. Attached you'll find the offer letter with the terms we discussed."

Dion didn't need to read anymore. He looked up, grinned and slapped Bobby on the shoulder. "Don't worry. I know exactly how to handle him."

Chapter Twenty-Eight

"Happy Valentine's Day, Vanessa!"

Vanessa looked up from the keys in her hand to her coworker Janice crossing the parking lot to her car. Vanessa smiled and waved. "Happy Valentine's Day to you, too."

Janice's straight dark hair still looked shiny and perfect despite their both arriving at the station at three in the morning for the morning news. Her eyes sparkled with joy and there was a bounce in her step. Not surprising since she carried a huge bouquet of roses with three heart balloons emblazoned with "Love You" and "Be Mine" attached to the vase by a long string.

Janice stopped in front of Vanessa's car. "Do you have any other stories to cover today?"

Vanessa shook her head. "No, I'm done for the day. What about you?"

Janice shook her head. "Nope. I asked for the rest of the day off. Mark made reservations at my favorite restaurant tonight and he told me he had a surprise." Janice's voice rose to an excited pitch. "I think he's finally going to propose!"

Vanessa grinned and shook her head. "Can you at least try to act surprised?"

Janice lifted a shoulder. "I'll try. His business finally turned a profit and he's hinting about settling down and starting a family. I'm sure that's what's going to happen."

"Text me and let me know. I'll cross my fingers and my toes."

Janice nodded enthusiastically. "You know it. What are you doing tonight? Isn't your boyfriend coming to town?"

The excitement Vanessa felt for Janice dimmed. "He's going to try. Now that he's got the offer with his brothers, they've been busy working out the deal with the studio and preparing to film their first episodes."

"Well, I'm going to believe he'll make it. That's exactly what Valentine's Day is for. A day to believe that love and happily-ever-afters exist."

"You're wasting your talents as a morning anchor. You really should start working for the card companies," Vanessa teased.

Janice chuckled. "Maybe I will. I'll see you tomorrow."

"Bright and early. Have a good night, and good luck."

Janice crossed her fingers, then went to her car. Vanessa got behind the wheel of her car and drove the short distance to her apartment. She rubbed her eyes and stifled her yawn with a hand over her mouth. It was only four in the afternoon, but all she wanted to do was go home, wash her face and crawl in the bed. She hadn't had the heart to tell Janice that Dion was not coming for Valentine's Day. He and his brothers had found themselves an agent who'd helped them navigate the contract for the show and a manager to guide them on the production process. Dion was busier than ever and between her schedule at the station, they were down to brief phone calls and video chats. He was in Atlanta with his brothers and said he would try to make it to Charlotte to see her for Valentine's Day, but she knew getting away would be difficult.

She arrived at her apartment a few minutes later and parked in the designated spot. She pulled out her cell phone as she got out of the car and called Dion. Even though she might not see him today, she wanted to talk to him before she washed up and climbed into bed. She didn't care if she was going to sleep early. She would have to be up at two in the morning in order to make it to the station by three.

His cell phone rang several times before voice mail picked up. The sound of his voice, even in a recording, brought a smile to her lips and made her heart ache. She missed him so much. "Hey, it's me. I'm off for the day and about to go inside and rest. Don't worry about waking me. Call me when you can. Love you."

With a sigh, she ended the call and made her way up the stairs to her apartment. She was just at her door when the door opposite of hers opened.

"Happy Valentine's Day, Vanessa."

Vanessa closed her eyes and sighed. Her neighbor, Tyler, hadn't done anything out of line or inappropriate, but she got the feeling he played nice-guy neighbor hoping to catch her in a weak moment. He was a chef at a restaurant and insisted on dropping off the extra food he just happened to make, helped her with groceries whenever he saw her carrying more than two bags, and offered to change the lightbulb in her entryway after noticing it flicker. He never hit on her when he helped, but the look in his eye said if she gave the go-ahead, he'd pounce.

She turned and plastered a tight smile on her face. "Hey, Tyler, happy Valentine's."

He strolled closer. "You just getting in from work?"

"Yep. It was a busy day today. I'm beat."

He nodded. "Any plans for tonight?"

She shook her head. "Nope. Just going to rest and get ready for tomorrow."

"Oh." His smile lifted. "I thought maybe your boyfriend was coming up."

She wasn't about to have a conversation about

Dion with Tyler. "What about you? Working or not? I bet the restaurant is busy with the holiday."

"I'm going in now. I made cheese tortellini last night. I can bring some over for you. That way you won't have to order in."

She waved a hand. "I'm good."

He patted his chest. "I want to. I'll pack some up for you and bring it over." He turned and went back into his apartment before she could reply.

Sighing, Vanessa unlocked her door and went into her apartment. Accepting the food was easier than arguing for ten minutes about not taking it. She kicked off her shoes and went into the living area and froze.

Dion's large body was spread out on her couch. He had one arm over his forehead covering his eyes, the other rested across his abdomen. His chest rose and fell in a slow rhythm. Vanessa dropped her purse and keys and rushed across the room.

He moved his arm and gave her a sleepy smile before she jumped on him.

"Oof," he said when she landed. His arms immediately wrapped around her. "Are you trying to kill me?"

"When did you get here? Why didn't you call me?"

His arms encircled her. "I wanted to surprise you. I got here about an hour ago."

"I didn't think you'd make it."

"Didn't I say I was coming?" He placed a hand behind her head and pulled her down for a kiss. "Happy Valentine's Day."

"You're the first person to say that who actually made me happy to hear it."

Dion sat up and Vanessa shifted to sit next to him. "Then I'm glad to be the one to tell you."

Vanessa wrapped her arms around his shoulders and breathed in the scent of him. If only he could be here every day when she got off work. If only she could feel his arms around her as she talked about the day and feel the vibration of his deep voice as she leaned against his chest. She'd gotten so used to having him beside her in the short time she'd spent in Sunshine Beach. They were making the long-distance thing work, but it wasn't the same as having him near.

"I missed you so much."

He kissed the top of her head. "I missed you, too. Which is why I think you're going to like my good news."

Her head popped up. "About the show?"

He shook his head. "Something else. I didn't want to say anything until I knew it was going to work out."

There was a knock on the door before he could continue. Vanessa sighed and rolled her eyes. "Sorry. That's probably Tyler. He insisted on bringing cheese tortellini for me."

She moved to get up, but Dion pressed a hand on her thigh. "I've got this." He walked to the door. Vanessa stayed on the couch and listened.

"Oh," came Tyler's surprised voice. "Vanessa didn't say you were here."

"I surprised her. Can I help you?"

A second of hesitation before Tyler spoke. "Yeah… I brought this over."

"Thanks. We'll enjoy it." The door closed a second later. Dion came back into the apartment and dropped the plastic container with the food on the coffee table.

"You took the food?"

"Hell yeah. If he's bringing it, I'm eating it. It's about time he learned that whatever he tries to do for you he'll have to do for both of us."

Her cheeks hurt from her grin. "Oh really?"

"Really." Dion sat next to her. "That's my good news. Tyler better get used to me be being here."

Vanessa's heart sped up. She slid closer to him. "You're going to be here?"

He nodded. "I am. I started looking for jobs in and around Charlotte right before you moved. I did a few interviews."

She slapped his chest. "You came here for interviews and didn't tell me."

Dion took her hand in his and placed it against the steady beat of his heart. "No, they were all virtual, which was why I worried, but I didn't have to. They offered me a position as public works director in the town next over. I accepted."

Vanessa hugged him. "That's fantastic."

"They are even okay with me having the series."

"Can you do both?"

"I'm going to try it out and see. I want both, and like you said, there's nothing wrong with going for what I want."

Vanessa's heart felt like it would explode with all of the happiness ballooning inside her. "So you're really going to be here. In Charlotte."

He pressed his forehead against hers before kissing her softly. "I really am. I guess I should find a place to stay."

She gripped his side. "Quit playing. You're moving in with me and that's the end of it."

He grinned. "Moving in with you until we find a place together."

A place together. Her heart melted. "What about the house in Sunshine Beach? I know you worked hard to keep it after your parents died."

He sighed and lifted a shoulder. "I'm not letting it go. Between Tyrone and Wes, it'll be taken care of. We'll find a way to make this work." He met her eyes. "Because I want to make this work. I'm ready to start the next chapter of my life. With you."

Vanessa leaned forward and kissed his cheek. "Thank you."

He frowned. "For what?"

"For being great. For not giving up on us when I moved. For always being supportive. For not only being a great boyfriend but giving my grandmother closure."

He ran his hands up her legs. "You don't have to thank me for any of that. Is your grandmother good?"

More than good. Her grandmother was thrilled to have found her ring. "Yep. She hasn't had any other strange things happening since the investigation. I guess that's all Granddad wanted."

He raised a brow. "So you believe in ghosts now?"

"I believe in miracles, and I guess that extends to the possibility that my grandfather's spirit helped my grandmother find her lost wedding ring."

He chuckled at her conciliatory tone. "After your adamant insistence that I was a fraud when we met, I'll take that."

"For real, thank you. You're great and I just want you to know I appreciate you."

"I love you, Vanessa. That's why I'll do all that I can for you. All I ask is to spend my life with you."

Vanessa smiled and kissed him. "All of this life and the next."

* * * * *

her shop to get a glimpse of her through the picture window. Talk about a glutton for punishment.

She let out a low growl. "You are an infuriating man. Stubborn and callous. I don't even know if you have a heart."

"Funny." He kept his voice steady even as memories flooded him, making his head pound. "That's the rationale Amber gave me for why she cheated with your fiancé. My lack of emotions pushed her into his arms. What was his excuse?"

She looked out at the street for nearly a minute, and Alex wondered if she was even going to answer. He followed her gaze to the park across the street, situated in the center of the town. There were kids at the playground and several families walking dogs on the path that circled the perimeter. Magnolia was the perfect place to raise a family.

If a person had the heart to be that kind of a man—the type who married the woman he loved and set out to be a good husband and father. Alex wasn't cut out for a family, but he liked it in the small coastal town just the same.

"I was too committed to my job," she said suddenly and so quietly he almost missed it.

"Ironic since it was your job that introduced him to Amber."

"Yeah." She made a face. "This is what I'm talking about, Alex. A past I don't want to revisit."

"Then stay away from me, Mariella," he advised. "Because I'm not going anywhere."

"Then maybe I will," she said and walked away.

Don't miss
Wedding Season *by Michelle Major,*
available May 2022 wherever
HQN books and ebooks are sold.

HQNBooks.com

SPECIAL EXCERPT FROM

HQN

Mariella Jacob was one of the world's premier bridal designers. One viral PR disaster later, she's trying to get her torpedoed career back on track in small-town Magnolia, North Carolina. With a second-hand store and a new business venture helping her friends turn the Wildflower Inn into a wedding venue, Mariella is finally putting at least one mistake behind her. Until that mistake—in the glowering, handsome form of Alex Ralsten—moves to Magnolia too...

Read on for a sneak preview of
Wedding Season,
the next book in USA TODAY *bestselling author Michelle Major's Carolina Girls series!*

"You still don't belong here." Mariella crossed her arms over her chest, and Alex commanded himself not to notice her body, perfect as it was.

"That makes two of us, and yet here we are."

"I was here first," she muttered. He'd heard the argument before, but it didn't sway him.

"You're not running me off, Mariella. I needed a fresh start, and this is the place I've picked for my home."

"My plan was to leave the past behind me. You are a physical reminder of so many mistakes I've made."

"I can't say that upsets me too much," he lied. It didn't make sense, but he hated that he made her so uncomfortable. Hated even more that sometimes he'd purposely drive by